A
Harlequin
Romance

OTHER
Harlequin Romances
by ELIZABETH ASHTON

Many of these titles are available at your local bookseller, or through the Harlequin Reader Service.

For a free catalogue listing all available Harlequin Romances, send your name and address to:

HARLEQUIN READER SERVICE,
M.P.O. Box 707, Niagara Falls, N.Y. 14302
Canadian address: Stratford, Ontario, Canada.

or use order coupon at back of book.

ALPINE RHAPSODY

by

ELIZABETH ASHTON

HARLEQUIN BOOKS

TORONTO
WINNIPEG

Original hard cover edition published in 1973
by Mills & Boon Limited

© Elizabeth Ashton 1973

SBN 373-01713-8

Harlequin edition published September 1973

Printed in Canada

1713

CHAPTER ONE

THE May sunshine poured into the *alm*, which formed a green oasis amidst the dark ranks of the conifers. The trees stretched beyond it, continuing their march up the hillside, thinning out as the slope became steeper, until it became so precipitous that they ceased altogether. A rough path crossed the *alm*, descending to the banks of a stream, where it broadened into a green ride. The stream ran down a narrow gorge, and eventually emptied itself into the lake in the valley. Through a break in the forest caused by the gorge, stark shapes of grey craggy heights still crowned with snow could be glimpsed against the azure sky.

The grass of the *alm* was studded with dark blue gentian flowers, and white wood sorrel grew where the trees began to impinge. In the shade, where the sun had not yet penetrated, was a large, flat rock, which provided a convenient resting place for walkers on their journey along the path which led to the mountain crest.

But no climber had availed himself of its invitation today. It was occupied by the drooping figure of a girl, who had no intention of going any further. She had come to the *alm* in search of solitude, and that she had found, for the place was quite deserted.

It was so quiet, and she sat so still, that a venturesome squirrel came within a few feet of her and a brown lizard came out upon a fallen tree trunk to enjoy the sun.

Evelyn Rivers saw neither the squirrel nor the lizard, and was impervious to the beauty around her. Her eyes were turned inwards towards the past, a past which even after two years still haunted her to the exclusion of her surroundings.

She wore upon her left hand a thin white glove, and obeying a sudden impulse, she stripped it off, and looked with repulsion at her hand, stretching the feeble white fingers. The top joint of her little finger was missing.

At the time of the accident, her friends, seeking to console her, had said:

'So lucky it was your left hand.'

But a pianist needed both her hands, and her playing had been her whole life.

She had been a rising star, her last concert had taken her almost to the top of the ladder. Vistas of international fame had opened before her. She had been hailed as brilliant, a genius, the most phenomenal female pianist of all time. Added to technical ability, she had a power and passion which brought the most hackneyed composition to new and vivid life. At last she had gained her reward for the long years of steady grind, though she had not grudged them, for from her childhood onwards she had spared no effort to develop her exceptional talent.

In her romantic teens, her own ordinary name had seemed too prosaic for the star which she was determined to become. She had called herself Evelina Ravelli, her dense black hair and classical features suggesting a Latin origin, which was not so. Harry had laughed at this pseudonym, saying it was pretentious, suggesting absurd alternatives, like Ripplena and Rallentanda. But Evelina Ravelli had been offered engagements all over Europe.

It was Harry's doing that she never fulfilled them, but he paid for his recklessness with his life.

Harry Travers had been a greater celebrity in his own line than she had yet become in hers, for he had arrived. A skiing champion, he had won cups and gold medals at

6

all the principal winter sports events. Handsome, adoring, he was everything that a girl could desire in a lover. But that last night they had quarrelled. He wanted her to give up her music and marry him at once, which she was loath to do. It was a most inopportune moment to re-open the matter, for he was taking her home after that so successful concert. She had been playing Liszt, a difficult composer, and the cadences from the Hungarian Rhapsodies were still running through her mind. Yet because she loved Harry, and wanted to make him a good wife, she was willing to compromise.

'Give me a year,' she had pleaded. 'Just one year to devote to my music, then I'll retire and marry you.'

'You needn't give it up entirely,' he had said condescendingly. 'There are always charity do's which would be glad of your services, but I don't think much of your idea of gadding around Europe for twelve months. Like as not you'd forget me.'

'You know I'd never do that, but I've worked so hard for success, haven't I the right to bring it to fulfilment before I settle down? Only a year, Harry.'

Harry was ardent and impatient, what he wanted he wanted at once, and he did not understand how important music was to her, nor did he realize in the least what a sacrifice she was prepared to make for him.

'I don't know what a piano's got that I haven't,' he grumbled. 'You're asking too much, Eve, I can't wait a whole year. I don't believe you love me at all.'

'Harry, I do – you know I do.'

He looked at her with eyes avid with desire.

'Then prove it. I know a good roadhouse near here. We'll tell your parents we had a breakdown ...' and as she made an involuntary movement of recoil. 'Eve, please!'

7

He had again chosen the wrong moment. Physically drained, she was still uplifted by her music, and in her exalted mood Harry's suggestion seemed like profanation. She had refused indignantly.

'Prudish, aren't you?' he had sneered, and had accelerated violently. When the crash came, Harry was killed and Evelyn's left hand was smashed.

At first there had been hope. Every possible treatment had been tried after the bones had set. A false joint had been fitted to her finger, which Evelyn finally tore off in a rage, when she realized that her hand would never regain its former suppleness and strength. Not only had she lost her lover, but her piano-playing days were done.

She had wanted to die, for it seemed to her that she had nothing left for which to live, but she was only twenty-five and healthy. She recovered physically from the double shock, but mentally she remained in a state of apathy, from which she refused to rouse herself.

Evelyn was the only child of well-to-do parents, who had never ceased to be astonished by the phenomenon which they had begotten. Her father liked a 'good tune', her mother was more musical, but they had never expected to produce a genius. Since it became apparent that they had done so, they did everything within their power to foster her talent, paying for the best teachers, and had been delighted by her success. They were delighted too when Harry Travers started paying her attention, he was so very eligible. She could so easily have fallen in love with some unstable musician. There had been a long-haired violinist who for a brief spell had been attracted, a young man without adequate means, but Evelyn's brief fancy for him soon evaporated.

With the loss of Harry, Evelyn had declared that her

heart was broken and she could never love again.

'Besides, who would want a cripple?' she had added bitterly, for her injury had reached colossal proportions in her morbid imagination.

'You're not crippled,' her father had told her patiently. 'It's not noticeable.'

She had refused to believe him and from that time forward she always wore a glove, which was only too obvious.

Her parents had been understanding and forbearing, but as the months went by and Evelyn made no effort to rouse herself or interest herself in anything, their patience began to wear thin.

'Leave me alone,' was her constant cry. 'Nothing matters to me any more.'

That spring, her father's sister, a widow, who assuaged her own loss with travel, had suggested taking Evelyn for an indefinite stay in the Tyrol.

'It's a beautiful country, and I know of a comfortable pension in Seefeld where I often stay,' she had told the Rivers. 'It's a healthy place, too, three thousand feet above sea level with mountains all around. There perhaps the poor child can find peace and healing.'

Since Evelyn was quite indifferent as to where she went or with whom, she accepted the offer with her usual listlessness. Amy Banks was older than her brother and had no children. A long widowhood had caused her to become a little spinsterish and old-fashioned. Evelyn considered that she was harmless and not likely to harass her with injunctions to 'snap out of it' as her father was beginning to do.

So Evelyn and Amy Banks came to the Tyrol.

It was beautiful, but its beauty made no impact upon Evelyn. She did not see it. Once beauty had made her

9

want to express her sensations in music, but that she could no longer do. In her despair she had repudiated music, she never listened to it if she could possibly avoid it. Mozart's country had nothing to say to her. Tactfully Amy made no references to Salzburg. That was a town they would not visit. Luckily it was a good many miles away.

Evelyn pulled on her glove again and sighed.

'Oh, Harry, Harry,' she said aloud. 'Why didn't you kill me too?'

The sun shone indifferently. Up in a bush a thrush began to sing. Evelyn flinched at the clear, pure notes. Tears welled up into her eyes and began to fall. Soon she was weeping copiously. She had not cried much since the accident, she had been too numb, her tragedy went too deep for tears, but something in the lushness of the spring, Nature's glad reawakening after the departure of the winter snows, touched some chord within her and loosened the floodgates of her grief.

The rattle of dislodged pebbles broke the silence, the squirrel streaked up the nearest tree, a flash of brown fur, the lizard flicked back into cover. Someone was coming down the path from the heights above. He came in sight, a lean, bronzed figure, a Tyrolean hat worn at a rakish angle on his fair head, forearms bare, below rolled-up shirt sleeves, neck also bare and brown showing above his open collar, but he wore strong shoes.

He stopped in surprise at the sight of the weeping Niobe upon her rock. Evelyn wore a short black skirt and a white blouse, her dense black hair was twisted into a braid over one shoulder; her ivory skin was not yet touched by the sun; she was a symphony in marble and ebony.

'*Grüss Gott, Fräulein,*' the newcomer greeted her

softly, and added something in German.

Evelyn started violently and raised her tear-stained face. Absorbed in her woe, she had been unaware of the stranger's approach. She met the bluest eyes that she had ever seen set in a lean, brown face. But this was no country yokel or tourist out on a ramble. In spite of his casual clothes, this man carried himself proudly and there was distinctionn about his straight features.

'*Ich verstehe nicht,*' she said. '*Englische.*'

It was the man's turn to start, and he stared at her intently.

'I must be dreaming,' he muttered in his own tongue. Then seeming to recollect himself, he extracted a clean, folded handkerchief from his back pocket, and held it out to her.

'Allow me,' he said in English. 'I know that the articles ladies use are inadequate for your present needs.' He had a pleasant cultivated voice with only a trace of accent, though his phraseology was a little formal. 'You weep because you have hurt yourself, or perhaps you are lost?' he suggested, while his eyes continued to study her face with an almost hungry look.

Evelyn took the handkerchief, unaware of his intent scrutiny, and mechanically wiped her face with it. It smelt of lavender.

'I'm both,' she said dramatically.

He raised a flaxen eyebrow.

'*Ach, so?* But you are not far from the town. You have but to follow the path and you will come to the main road. But if you are hurt, perhaps you cannot walk?' He glanced down at her feet encased in flimsy white sandals. 'Those little things are most pretty, but not suitable for hillside walking. You twist the ankle?'

Against her will, Evelyn actually laughed. There was

11

something a little comical about the stranger's serious concern regarding a non-existent injury. It was the first time that she had laughed for many a long day.

'I'm afraid I misled you,' she explained. 'I . . . I'm quite all right really. It's only . . .' Her voice died away and her momentary interest died. Her expression became aloof and sombre as was habitual with her. 'I came here to be alone,' she added pointedly.

'It is not good to be alone so that one must weep,' he told her. He looked at the flower-studded grass. 'Permit me?'

Not understanding his intention, she nodded slightly, and he stretched himself at her feet.

Evelyn made an instinctive gesture of recoil; she always shrank from encounters with strangers and this one seemed to be preparing for a long stay. She made a half movement to rise, but checked it. She had nothing to do if she did go away and she could easily snub him if he became too curious.

'I have been up on the Reitherspitze,' he remarked. 'It is quite a long walk.'

'Is that the mountain above us?' she asked indifferently.

'Yes, but it is not one of the high ones, and I cheated. I went up in the *seilbahn* and walked across from the Ros-shutte. There is still a lot of snow up there.'

'I suppose so.' She had not noticed, though the summit was clearly visible on fine days. Involuntarily, her eyes were drawn to the long, lean figure lying in the grass. He was a very good-looking specimen, but she had no further interest in men, whatever they looked like. She wondered why he had stayed to talk to her. She could not present a very prepossessing figure. Her clothes were not smart and she must appear worse than usual after her tears.

He had pulled his hat over his eyes to shield them from the sun, but from the shade of its brim he was still studying her closely.

'You stay in Seefeld?' he asked. 'I think I have seen you somewhere.'

'That's unlikely, the place is becoming thronged with tourists, and I keep out of the town.'

'Perhaps it was not in Seefeld.'

She eyed him warily. She had no desire to meet any acquaintance from the past.

'I'm sure you can't have done,' she said firmly.

'May I know your name?'

'Certainly, it's Rivers. Eve Rivers.'

He looked disappointed. 'I do not know it.'

'Of course not. I've never seen you in my life before.' She was emphatic.

'*Ach so.* But you have some great sorrow? That is why you sit alone here and weep?'

Evelyn had no intention of telling him her history. It was unfortunate that he had discovered her in her moment of weakness, but that did not give him the right to probe.

'That's my affair,' she said coldly.

'And I am too inquisitive?' He smiled charmingly. 'But on such a lovely day, no one should weep. It is a privilege to be alive.'

'I don't think so,' she cried violently, 'and I prefer rain to sunshine.'

He sat up, pushing back the hat from his eyes and looked at her reproachfully.

'But, Fräulein Rivers, such a pronouncement amounts to blasphemy! God gave us the beautiful earth, the trees and the flowers to solace our ills, and sunshine is too rare to be scorned. You are young, you have all your senses,

13

you are in a beautiful place and not in want. Are not all these blessings something for which to render thanks?'

'When there are many other people worse off – why don't you finish the cliché?' she asked scornfully. 'But do you think that reflection ever really comforted anybody for a personal tragedy?'

'It should help.'

'Well, it doesn't, and when I want a sermon, I go to church.'

A little colour had risen in her cheeks and her dark eyes sparkled. Though it was only resentment which she felt, he had managed to pierce her normal apathy. The effect was magical, she was a statue coming to life.

'So you attend the *kirche*?' he asked, and she flushed, for she had not been to a service since her tragedy, feeling God had deserted her.

His eyes were quizzical, but their expression changed to admiration, as he noted the length of her long, silky lashes, as she looked down at her hands folded in her lap, the cameo delicacy of her features against the dark background of trees behind her.

'You have loved and lost?' he hazarded.

With her gaze still upon her hands, she said dramatically:

'My heart is dead.'

He suppressed a smile. He had heard that statement from girls before and a few months later they had married someone else.

'Nothing ever really dies,' he told her gently. He indicated the gentians. 'Every winter those flowers die, but each spring they reappear. Your heart will reawaken.'

'I don't want it to,' she cried passionately. 'I should only suffer again.'

'*Ach*, but that is life. It is better to suffer than to be

14

atrophied, and if there is pain there is also ecstasy.'

'Not for me.' Her hands went to clasp her throat. 'I shall never feel ecstasy again.' The glove was very noticeable and the stranger eyed it curiously.

'Never is a long time, Fräulein Rivers. May I ask how old you are?'

Mechanically she told him, her thoughts far away.

'Twenty-five!' he exclaimed. 'That is no age at all. You are not yet fully mature. Believe me, *Fräulein*, you will have joy again, if you cease to skulk behind your grief. That is being cowardly.'

Evelyn's eyes flashed with indignation. Throughout her months of mourning, she had behaved with dignity and restraint. She had not sought to unload her sorrow on to others. All she had asked was to be left alone ... entirely alone. And yet this man, this stranger, who had thrust himself upon her, had not only presumed to lecture her, but he had called her a coward.

Without deigning to make any rejoinder, she rose to her feet.

'I must be going,' she said.

With a swift, lithe movement he sprang up from the grass. She realized then that he was a good head taller than herself, and she was a tall girl. She knew a moment's satisfaction; his height made her feel feminine, small men embarrassed her – a woman should look up to a man, not down. Instantly she reacted from her thought. What did it matter if he were tall, short or a hunchback? She was entirely indifferent.

'I may accompany you?' he asked.

'I would prefer to go alone.'

His mouth set in an obstinate line. This was a man who was not easily gainsaid.

'Nevertheless, I will see you safely to the road.'

She shrugged her shoulders helplessly. 'I can't prevent you.'

The downward path was steep and scattered with loose stones. When the snows had melted it had been a cataract, and as he had said, her sandals were unsuitable footwear for such terrain. Anxious to assert her independence, she went too fast and carelessly. She slipped, stumbled and would have fallen but for his restraining hand upon her arm.

'Careful, *Fräulein*, permit me.' He drew her right arm through his. 'Lean upon me.'

She was startled by his action. His close proximity, the contact with his bare, muscular arm beneath her hand brought an awareness of his masculine virility to senses that had been suppressed far too long. Hers was a warm and passionate nature which had been frozen by grief. Now as the May sunshine was thawing the last lingering snows of winter from the mountain summits, her pulses leaped at the resurgence of new life.

The realization that sensuous feeling was not dead gave her a shock, but her sensations were not unpleasant. That gave her a further shock. She had always been so absorbed in her music that Harry's were the first male caresses she had known – the violinist had never ventured further than kissing her hand. Innocently she had surmised that because she still loved Harry's memory, no other man could stir her. She glanced almost fearfully at her companion's profile. He was staring straight ahead of them with a little furrow between his brows as if in deep thought and seemed completely unconscious of her and the effect he was having upon her. She was piqued.

'Do you make a habit of it?' she asked abruptly.

'Of what, *Fräulein*?'

'Playing knight errant to damsels in distress.'

He smiled. He really had a charming smile, she conceded unwillingly.

'Alas, it is not often my good fortune to meet with one, and certainly I have never met one as beautiful as yourself.'

'Rubbish,' she said energetically, 'I'm not beautiful.'

'Allow me to disagree. You are more so than most, and yours is a beauty which will never die. You have such perfect bone structure.'

'Don't, you make me feel like a skeleton!' she exclaimed, laughing.

'But we have put the skeletons in the cupboard.'

She was silent, realizing that twice that morning she had laughed, who never thought to laugh again. But it would take more than his flattery and charm to dissipate her melancholy. She did not even want it to be dissipated.

They had reached the ravine which housed the stream. Higher up the mountain, it fell in a torrent, but below the path, it was no more than a gentle trickle, meandering along its boulder-strewn course. The bank dropped steeply down to it, and the forest rose again on the further bank. Here the path broadened and its surface was smoother, so that Evelyn had no further need of suppport. She withdrew her hand from his arm, saying coldly:

'Thank you, I can manage now.'

Her companion glanced at her averted face, but made no comment.

The path became a lane which wound through the last of the forest, beech trees and holm oak mingled with the firs. On a tree stump near the verge, husk of fir cones indicated a squirrel's dining table. The man pointed it out.

'Very interesting,' she remarked in a bored tone.

She became aware that she was still carrying his handkerchief crumpled up in her left hand, and it was damp with her tears. Looking at it ruefully, she told him:

'I must return your property, but I'll have it washed first.'

'You cannot do that, for you do not know what I am called, nor my address,' he reminded her, a faint reproach sounding in his voice. 'You have not been interested enough to ask.'

'There was no occasion to do so, was there?' she said crushingly. 'But now there is, what is it?'

'My name is Maximilian Linden,' he informed her, and looked at her inquiringly.

Seeing the question in his eyes, she asked indifferently:

'Should I have heard of it?' for it conveyed nothing to her.

'*Ach, nein, Fräulein*, I do not flatter myself that it is known outside Austria.' But she sensed that he was somehow disappointed. However, she was not going to gratify him by asking what he did.

'Naturally my somewhat pretentious name is shortened to Max,' he went on, 'and as such I am known to my friends.'

'Naturally, Herr Linden,' she agreed, ignoring the insinuation. She had no intention of calling him Max.

'My home is in Vienna.' Again the questioning look, but as she made no comment, he went on to explain that he was on vacation is Seefeld.

'I often stay in the Tyrol, because it is a country that has a very great appeal to me, and I have many friends in the vicinity.'

He mentioned that he was staying at one of the more

superior hotels, one which Evelyn had seen and knew was a gay place.

'Do none of your many friends like climbing?' she asked carelessly, since he appeared to be alone.

'*Ach so*, but there are time when one's own company is best.'

'Quite,' she said dryly.

'But not if one is going to weep.'

She ignored that, and he swooped forward to take the handkerchief from her slack fingers.

'It is not necessary for you to burden yourself with the laundering of my handkerchief. It is honoured to have dried your tears.'

Too flowery altogether, she thought disdainfully, while instinctively she tried to conceal her hand in a fold of her skirt, but of course he was a foreigner. His eyes were again questioning her, and she realized that he must have noticed the glove, and was too polite to mention it. She said nothing.

They had reached the road and he had no excuse to linger.

'Here we part,' she said firmly. 'Thanks for everything, Herr Linden, including the lecture. I don't suppose that we'll meet again.' Unexpectedly she felt a faint regret.

'But I hope that we will.'

'There's no harm in hoping,' she said flippantly.

'I shall endeavour to ensure that we do,' he told her significantly.

She said nothing to that, merely raising her level brows.

'And because I am sure that we shall, I shall only say *auf wiedersehen*, Eve, which means until we see each other again.'

He had so far forgotten himself to use her first name.

'Good-bye, Herr Linden,' she said mockingly, and ran across the road. She had half expected he would follow her, but when from a safe distance upon the farther side, she looked back, there was no sign of him.

Evelyn's way led her past a shallow lake, the Wildsee, upon which pleasure-seekers were disporting themselves in sturdy boats. On the farther side of the lake rose a green mound, spangled with flowers, beyond it were wooded hills, above which the Hohe Munde reared its rounded head, and to the right of it the range of the Wetterstein showed a succession of jagged peaks. At the end of the lake, the road entered the town, where the red spire of the church, chief landmark in Seefeld, thrust a pointed finger into the sky. Evelyn paused and drew a deep breath. For the first time she was looking at her surroundings with a seeing eye, and realized that they were incredibly beautiful. The beauty made her heart ache with active pain; if only Harry had been there to share it with her! The hard shell of her grief had been pierced by a pair of vivid blue eyes, and as when circulation is restored to a frozen limb, she was suffering the pangs of returning life. She was not grateful to Max for inaugurating the process, which he had undoubtedly done. Vainly she clutched at the mummy-like swathings of her grief in which she had sought to hide herself from any contact with the living world, but it was useless. They were slipping away from her and new life was stirring within her, life which might bring fresh suffering, and she had hoped never to suffer again.

Except along its main street, the houses in Seefeld are not arranged in rows, but are scattered haphazardly among its green spaces and clumps of birch tree saplings, pretty graceful trees, which had been planted in odd corners. The pension where Amy Banks and her niece were staying was back from the main road, and approached on two sides by narrow lanes. The open space of green field before it was probably designed for a building site, but in the meantime it afforded a view of the green mound on the way to the lake, and the steep fir-lined slope of the Geschwandtkopfhutt to the left, which in winter was a ski-run. A modern house, it was built in the usual type of Tyrolean architecture – deep-eaved roof sheltering the balconies which ran round outside the windows of the first and second floors. It was painted white and called Haus Clara, and was approached by a short flight of steps made out of slabs of slate which led on to a small terrace outside the front door, on which was a table and chairs.

Inside, a few steps down on the left led into the spacious dining-room, with walls of polished wood. Wood predominated in all the Tyrolean decoration schemes, often the whole top storey being composed of it, and since the area abounded in forests, this was not surprising. The smaller lounge was to the right of the front door, with an upholstered bench running round it beneath the two windows and a small bar at one end. A curved staircase ascended to the first floor, where Evelyn and Amy had adjoining rooms, both opening on to the balcony.

Upon Evelyn's return from her walk, she found her aunt reclining in a deck chair outside her bedroom window enjoying the sunshine and the view of the distant mountains. She was knitting, for this craft was her invariable occupation. Socks, scarves and sweaters came into being under her busy fingers, and her friends and relatives were presented with many tokens of her energy.

Evelyn looked down at her aunt's recumbent figure,

thinking that up to now she had taken Amy and her kindnesses very much for granted. This was another bonus for which she had so far shown little gratitude, and she ought to make an effort to be more sociable.

Amy was not really old, though not being strong, she had acquired elderly habits. Her hair had turned prematurely white, but her skin had a pink and white delicacy, while the grey eyes, which looked up at Evelyn kindly, were shrewd.

'Had a nice walk?' she asked chattily, noticing with pleasure that her niece looked more animated than usual, and hoped fervently that the change was beginning to do her good. 'Where did you go?'

'The usual place, up to the Reith Alm. It's so quiet and peaceful there.'

'All alone? I know I'm not much of a walker, but there are many pleasant people staying here. Surely one of them would have liked to go with you?'

'I don't want them, and they don't want me,' Evelyn returned. 'Most of them prefer more exciting diversions, boating, swimming or excursions.'

She sat down on another canvas chair and her gaze went to the mountains. Amy's eyes dwelt lovingly upon the girl's pale face, half obscured by the fall of black hair.

'Wouldn't you like to go on an excursion?' she suggested hopefully. 'There are many interesting places to see.'

Evelyn shook her head. 'I hate travelling around in herds. You know I prefer to be alone.'

'But it's so bad for you to be always alone,' Amy sighed.

Evelyn's dark eyes came back from the mountains with a spark of mischief in their depths.

'As it happens I wasn't alone this morning. I was picked up by a man.'

'Oh dear!' Consternation showed on Amy's face. 'How very trying. Whatever did you do?'

For the third time that day, Evelyn laughed.

'Actually it was rather amusing,' she said. 'He was quite a respectable young man, and not so very young, now I come to think of it.' Her eyebrows puckered as she tried to recall Max's appearance. There had been an assurance about him which implied maturity. 'He gave me a lecture,' she went on, 'told me that I ought to count my blessings.'

'But surely . . .' Amy began, for it was inconceivable that Evelyn would have confided her trouble to a stranger. 'What made him do that?' she asked doubtfully.

'Seemed to think I didn't appreciate the beauties of Seefeld,' Evelyn said offhandedly. 'And I haven't up to now, nor your kindness in bringing me here.' She looked affectionately at her aunt.

'That's all right, I'm glad of your company,' Amy told her, secretly immensely gratified that Evelyn seemed more human. 'But this man, you've no idea who he was?'

'Well, he did tell me his name was Max Linden and he came from Vienna,' Amy started. 'But that conveyed nothing to me except that he was Austrian.'

Amy stopped knitting. 'And that was all?' she asked in a strained voice.

Evelyn was frowning. 'Come to think of it, the name does ring a faint bell.' She shook her head. 'But no, I'm sure I've never met him before. I couldn't forget him if I had.'

Amy looked at her with interest. So she had found Max

Linden attractive! That was a big step forward, but if Max was who she thought he might be, he was a dangerous associate for her niece in her present state.

'Did you arrange a further meeting?' she asked anxiously.

'Oh no, it was just a casual encounter,' Evelyn said lightly. 'He was coming down and found me half-way up. So we came back together.'

She did not think it was necessary to confess that Max had found her in tears.

Amy sighed with relief. 'That's a good thing,' she said. 'I mean, you don't know anything about him or whether he's . . . er . . . to be trusted.'

'Don't be so old-fashioned,' Evelyn cried impatiently. 'Nowadays men and girls don't wait for formal introductions. Am I expected to present my friends to be vetted by my relations?'

But Max was not a friend nor likely to become one. She did not take his insistence that they would meet again seriously. It was in keeping with his flowery compliments, and he had probably already forgotten her. The thought caused her to feel despondent. For the first time since her tragedy, she realized that she was lonely.

'Of course I don't expect any such thing,' Amy said a little sharply, for she prided herself upon her modern outlook. 'But all the same, you must be careful with foreigners. He might have become . . . er . . . fresh. Is that the right word?'

'Not as applied to him,' Evelyn told her, smiling. 'He was perfectly polite and correct.' She glanced at her watch. 'It's nearly lunch time and I must wash my hands.'

As she turned towards her own room, Amy called after her, 'Did you tell him your name?'

Evelyn swung back. 'You don't suppose that would convey anything to him, do you?'

'No, of course not,' Amy agreed. She had momentarily forgotten that the musical world knew her niece as Evelina Ravelli. There would be nothing to connect Evelyn Rivers with her past. As the girl disappeared, Amy let her knitting fall into her lap. She was particularly anxious her niece should not encounter any echo from her former days which might retard her recovery. Music and all things musical had become taboo in conversation with her, but an outsider would not know that.

It was fortunate that Evelyn did not remember Max Linden's name, but not surprising; there had been so many applications for her services, it might not have registered.

But Amy remembered the letter which had been forwarded by Evelyn's agent. Proud of her niece's success, she had been excited by every offer and her brother had shown it to her. For Max Linden was an important personage in continental musical circles. He was connected with several concert halls in Bavaria and Austria and was at present engaged as Musical Director at the Mozart Opera House in Vienna.

Impressed by reports of Ravelli's talent, he was inquiring if she would contemplate coming to Austria. Before that letter could be answered, Evelyn's public life had ended and he had been informed that she was not available.

However, it was improbable that this could be the same Max Linden, for such a notable character would surely be quite elderly and not given to roaming about on mountain tops, and even if he were it was still more improbable that he would connect Evelyn Rivers with the glamorous Ravelli. He had never seen Evelina, and her niece looked very different now, though she had appeared better and brighter that morning.

Amy was anxious that no reverberations from the past should disturb their holiday, and the mention of Max Linden's name had aroused unwelcome speculations, but after all, Evelyn had assured her that it was unlikely that she would encounter him again.

Assuring herself that her fears were groundless, Amy bundled up her knitting and went to join her niece for lunch.

CHAPTER TWO

THE clientele at Haus Clara was neither smart nor distinguished, comprising an ordinary assortment of visitors, which changed every one or two weeks. The collection normally included elderly couples, female pairs, a sprinkling of youngsters and one or two families with children. Finding them all uninspiring, Evelyn had ignored them as far as was compatible with politeness, in fact she barely noticed them. They were mere shadows making no impression.

Today, being a little more conscious of her surroundings, she noticed several empty tables as she took her seat and remarked upon it to her aunt.

'Yes, the Colmers have gone, and the Weston family.' Amy was more cognizant of her neighbours, 'but there'll be another flight in this afternoon, I understand. The place is filling up for the summer season, though I believe it's even more crowded during the winter sports months.'

Evelyn winced at the mention of winter sports. Harry had been to Innsbruck to ski, but not if she remembered aright to Seefeld. She visualized the landscape covered in snow and shivered. She supposed that by the time next winter came, she would have had to make up her mind as to what she was to do with the rest of her life, and the long, empty years stretched bleakly ahead of her. Max had reminded her that she was young and had the use of her faculties, but the prospect of going out into the world to find some suitable occupation appalled her. She had never wanted to do anything except play the piano, but presumably she could teach since she knew a great deal about music, but few people bothered to learn the pianoforte nowadays and the sight of the once well-loved instrument caused her pain.

Amy noticed that the brooding look had returned to her face and said brightly:

'Perhaps the next contingent will produce someone really interesting.'

'I think that's most unlikely,' Evelyn returned indifferently.

In the afternoon they pottered round the shops, dropped into a café for coffee and cakes and took a stroll along the wooded path on the far side of the Wildsee. It was their usual programme and Evelyn had accepted it without question. Today she felt bored with it; she knew every inch of the path along the lake side, and even the antics of several tame squirrels failed to distract her. She suggested that they might go upon an excursion after all and see something of the country.

Amy was delighted by this change of front. They would that evening see what the hotel had to offer. There were many exciting places to visit – the Bavarian lakes, St. Anton, the Dolomites, or nearer at hand Innsbruck. Evelyn listened, already regretting her impulsive suggestion. Such a trip meant travelling in a bus or coach which she disliked, but having roused her aunt's expectations, she would have to go through with it.

They returned in time for dinner. Visitors at Haus Clara did not dress for this meal, though some of the older ones changed from sports wear into more formal attire. Evelyn, out of deference to her aunt, usually put on a long frock. That night she selected a grey silk garment – she had not worn colours since Harry's death – which clung to her too thin figure like a sheath. It gave her a slightly spectral appearance, which up to now had suited her mood. She had deliberately fostered a wraith-like image, for she was only the ghost of her former self. But tonight she surveyed her reflection with slight scorn, thinking that she was becoming something of a poseur. She searched through her wardrobe, looking for a bright scarf or shawl to relieve the dreary effect, but she possessed nothing coloured. She had thrown out all bright things.

The lights were coming on in the town and the mountains were veiled in twilight as they finished dinner. Most of the guests would be going out to the various diversions offered to them. Seefeld boasted a night club and a casino. The Haus Clara did not provide either a radio or a television set, since its visitors usually went out, but aunt and niece spent their evenings in the lounge, occasionally taking a short stroll outside if the night were fine and warm. Their only diversion was an occasional glass of wine.

As the lounge emptied, Evelyn tried to settle to a book, while Amy knitted, but she felt restless. Their evening routine was more suited to an old woman than a girl of twenty-five. She scolded herself for the thought; there was nothing that she wanted to do and nobody to do it with if there were.

It was very quiet. Occasionally someone came in for a drink, and their host emerged from the back regions to pour it. No one took any notice beyond a formal greeting of the two women seated over by the window. The sound of a car stopping outside was unremarkable. Several of the guests had brought their cars.

A man came into the lounge, giving a swift look round. He smiled when he saw Evelyn. He was very perfectly groomed in a dark suit, his unruly fair hair neatly plastered down, and he had vivid blue eyes. Evelyn gave a gasp.

'Max Linden!' she whispered to Amy. 'But how on earth?'

Amy looked at him and her heart sank. This man could very well be the musical director. His grooming, his assured air were that of a man of the world.

Max bowed to Evelyn.

'*Grüss Gott, Fräulein*,' he said pleasantly. 'May I get you a drink?' Without waiting for her reply, he went to the counter and tapped impatiently upon it. 'That is if there is anyone here to provide it.'

Amy looked taken aback, but Evelyn answered:

'Thank you, since you are so kind. The regulars usually shout down the passage for attention.'

Though she spoke gravely, her eyes were alight with mischief. She had wanted a diversion and since one had presented itself, she did not intend to let it escape. Max was obviously used to more ambitious hostelries and deplored the lack of service at the Haus Clara. However, at that moment Herr Hofman came hurrying in, bowing obsequiously to the newcomer and addressing him in German.

'Sherry?' Max suggested, and at their murmured thanks, ordered it and a schnapps for himself. The drinks poured and paid for, he brought them over and seated himself opposite to them across the small table which was between them.

'So we meet again as I foretold,' he said to Evelyn.

'But how did you know I was staying here?' Evelyn inquired, wondering if he had combed the innumerable hotels and pensions in search of her. The idea was flattering and a little flutter of excitement stirred her pulses as she met his eyes.

'Instinct led me in the right direction,' he said airily, 'or whatever it is that guides a homing pigeon. I was driving by and saw you through the window.'

Evelyn glanced involuntarily at the big window, with its undrawn curtains, but she knew he could not have been driving by, for no road led past the Haus Clara. Both the lane approaches ended in a cul-de-sac. However, she decided not to point that out. Not until long afterwards did he confess that he had trailed her to the hotel, keeping well out of her sight, and had decided to call that evening.

She was a little at a loss to account for his continued interest. She was no longer a famous pianist, and she had lost her looks and her bloom, or so it seemed to her, nor had she been specially forthcoming when she had met him on the *alm*. She had nothing with which to attract a good-looking and apparently affluent foreigner, and there must be many more alluring women staying at the expensive hotel where he was lodging.

But Amy was on tenterhooks, wondering if he had recognized her niece, and when he innocently asked if Evelyn had recovered from her indisposition, she jumped, thinking he was referring to her accident, but when he concluded with, 'of this morning', her anxiety was turned to reproach.

'Weren't you well?' she asked Evelyn. 'You never said anything.'

'It wasn't anything,' Evelyn murmured, aware that she had blushed.

'Fräulein Eve is perhaps not yet used to our mountain air,' Max said suavely. 'It is fortunate that I was passing and was able to assist her.'

Amy glanced from the serenely smiling man to the embarrassed girl, surmising that Evelyn had not told her all

31

that had transpired during their meeting.

'I'm sure Eve is grateful to you,' she said doubtfully, and Max laughed.

'Far from it,' he said with a glint in his eyes. 'I took the opportunity to give her some advice, which I think did not please her at all.'

'It was presumptuous,' Evelyn told him.

'*Ach*, no, it was not meant so,' he assured her. He glanced at Amy. 'But you have not introduced me.'

'My aunt, Mrs. Banks,' Evelyn said frigidly. 'Herr Linden.'

He stood up, bowed, and sat down again. 'Delighted to meet you, madam. Will you not have another drink?'

'No, thank you,' Amy said quickly, 'I never take more than one glass of wine.' She was still eyeing him nervously.

'Very abstemious. Eve ...' he dropped the Fräulein, 'will you not have something more? A cherry brandy?'

Evelyn declined. 'It's very nice of you to have called,' she said in a tone which suggested just the opposite. 'But it really wasn't necessary.'

She played with the stem of her wine glass, wishing that he would not stare at her so fixedly. He was quite disturbingly attractive, but his behaviour was bordering upon impertinence. He was almost forcing himself upon her, and she had indicated when she parted from him that she did not expect to see him again. True, she had then felt a faint regret, but now some instinct was warning her that no good could come from further association.

'That is a matter of opinion,' he said dryly, and she raised her eyebrows.

'What do you mean?'

'That as you have cast me in the role of knight errant, I

am only living up to my part.'

'But I'm no longer in distress,' she said quickly.

His eyes held hers with meaning in their depths.

'Are you not?' he asked quietly.

She looked away uneasily. 'Of course not.'

Having no key to their conversation, Amy was also looking uneasy, wondering what their visitor might say next.

'My niece was in need of rest and quiet,' she said to explain their presence in Seefeld. 'We are finding both here, and I think the change is doing her good.'

'A little too quiet perhaps,' he suggested. 'Young girls need recreation. Roaming about the hillsides alone is not very gay.'

'I don't want gaiety, and I enjoy my own company,' Evelyn said repressively.

'Indeed? Were you enjoying it when I came upon you?' he asked wickedly.

'Oh, really!' Evelyn exclaimed angrily. 'Can't you forget about that?'

'No,' he said simply. 'It made too deep an impression.'

'But what was Eve doing?' Amy demanded anxiously.

'Crying,' Evelyn told her shortly.

'Oh dear!' Amy looked in consternation at Max. She herself had never seen Evelyn cry, she did not know if it was a good sign or a bad one, but what deductions had he drawn from her tears?

Evelyn was in a state of conflict. One half of her was resenting Max's intrusion, wanting only to creep back into the cocoon of her retirement, the other, the resurgence of her youth, was clamouring that here was opportunity, a gateway back to the living world which she had eschewed so long. But did she want to go back?

Could she return to what she had once been? Her eyes fell upon her left hand. She could not. Evelina Ravelli was extinguished, and without her music she was a lost being.

She looked up and saw Max was watching her intently with a slightly mocking gleam in his eyes, deriding her despondency. He did not know about Evelina, he should never know.

'I've changed my mind,' she said defiantly, feeling that some stimulant would help her to cope with him. 'I would like another drink, please.'

'Good. I will have *mein Herr* concoct for you a speciality of my own.'

What was in it besides the tinkling ice, she did not know. Thinking about it later, she decided it had been liberally laced with vodka, for its action was delayed. As she sipped it, he asked casually:

'Do you dance?'

'Dance?' She stared at him blankly.

'A common diversion among young people,' he explained. 'And a pleasant form of exercise.'

'Of course I know that. I don't dance.'

'What a pity!' He glanced at her supple figure. 'But perhaps you could learn?'

She laughed at the absurd notion. She was an excellent dancer, it had been one of hers – and Harry's – favourite recreations.

'I mean I don't dance now,' she told him.

'Why not? I think it would do you much good.' He glanced at his watch. 'It is still quite early. There is dancing at my hotel tonight. Will you not come?'

'Now? With you?'

'I would esteem it an honour.'

She had a brief vision of bright lights and whirling

couples, the intoxication of moving in rhythm to lilting tunes, not her kind of music, that she never wanted to hear again, but superficial easy stuff. It would be good to dance again, but only with Harry – and there was no Harry.

'Come,' he said coaxingly, 'it will be a change for you. Just for a little while, you need not stay long,' and added meaningly: 'It will help to break the ice.'

What was he talking about? What ice? Ice tinkled in her glass as she drained it. The potent stuff was going to her head. Through a rising mist, she saw his eyes, very blue and insistent, fixed upon hers, willing her to come. Not wholly aware of what she was doing, she rose to her feet and moved uncertainly round the table towards him. He drew her arm through his, and laughed triumphantly. Evelyn laughed too, recklessly.

'Eve, should you?' Amy protested. 'You aren't . . .'

Max interrupted her. 'Mrs. Banks, please, leave this to me. I only seek to do her good.'

Quelled by his authoritative air, Amy subsided. Max led Evelyn out of the lounge, down the steps, and put her into his car.

The hotel was only a short distance away. The dance floor, when they entered the room, was dimly lit and a waltz had just begun, a Strauss waltz. The management that evening were paying tribute to the Viennese musician.

Evelyn faltered as the familiar strains registered, she had steadfastly refused to listen to any music for so long, but they only added to the complete unreality of what was happening. Max drew her into his arms and glided away with her. Mechanically she responded to the rhythm. She seemed to have stepped back in time, the past two years slipped away like an evil phantasma. In her vague dreamy state, tonight was a repetition of many similar nights, when she had danced to sensuous music in a man's arms. Her senses were alert if her mind was befogged. Instinctively she raised her face, and laid her smooth cheek against her partner's.

'Oh, Harry, it's good to be with you again!' she murmured.

Max said nothing, but gathered her a little closer in his hold. A muscle in his cheek twitched. This was not the reaction which he had expected. He realized he must have overdone the vodka.

The dance ended, the lights turned up. The mixed crowd of performers, in clothes ascending from the casual to evening dress, glanced curiously at the distinguished-looking man and the tall, slender girl in clinging grey. Max Linden most of them knew, and they smiled and nodded to him, but Evelyn received only stares, hostile from the women, inquisitive from the men. Where had Max Linden picked up this strange-looking girl, who looked half dazed?

Max hurriedly swept Evelyn out on to a wide terrace to which the room had access, not wishing to be accosted. He allowed her to sink down into a wicker chair and stood beside her. It was cool and dark, the sky above them spangled with stars. The fresh air cleared Evelyn's head. She looked around her at the unfamiliar scene, realizing that the man beside her was not Harry, realizing also what she had done. In a low, choked voice, she told him:

'I'll never forgive you for this – ever!'

'I did nothing. I only sought to give you pleasure,' he said gently.

'You made me drunk ... I didn't know what I was doing.'

'You were only a little elevated,' he excused her. 'I did not realize that you would not be used to alcohol.'

'It was unpardonable . . . I . . . I was awful!' She twisted her hands together in her lap, remembering how she had put her cheek against his.

'You were charming,' he said gravely.

She stood up unsteadily. 'I would like to go now.'

'As you wish.'

He offered her his arm and she had perforce to take it, for she was still unsure of her balance. Contact with him was repugnant to her, she thought wildly – only it was not. Again she was reminded of Harry. How she had missed a man's protective presence. Harry had always been ready with the small courtesies which mean so much to women – women like herself, who were too feminine to wish to assert their independence. She liked being assisted into cars, having doors opened for her, being waited upon, a strong arm to lean upon. It made her feel rare and precious. Max's arm was strong and muscular, but he was not Harry.

In silence he guided her out of the hotel and back to his car. She stood quietly beside him while he unlocked it, drawing in deep breaths of the night air. Her head cleared entirely and she regained the control of her limbs. When he opened the door for her, she sprang inside without his help.

As he took his place beside her, she said politely:

'I'm sorry, I should not have spoken as I did. You've been very kind.'

He asked, as he started the engine,

'Who is Harry?'

The familiar name on his lips gave her a slight shock. No one had dared to mention Harry Travers to her during the past two years. Shock was followed by panic.

She had spoken the beloved's name aloud; how much else had she given away? Not much, she supposed, since he had asked not who was Harry, but who *is* he.

'A friend,' she said vaguely.

He gave her a keen glance, but said no more.

He pulled up at the Haus Clara. Amy was standing on the terrace above the steps peering anxiously into the night. She gave a sigh of relief as Evelyn came towards her, and she searched the girl's face seeking for signs of strain, but Evelyn was perfectly composed, her features set in their usual immobility.

'Good night, Herr Linden,' she said coldly. 'Thank you for the entertainment. Coming up, Auntie?'

'In a minute,' Amy told her, 'I must fetch my knitting from the lounge.' She had left it there, when she had run out upon hearing the car stop.

Evelyn went upstairs without looking back. Amy and Max watched her until she was out of sight. Then they looked at each other and Max asked the question he had already asked the niece:

'She spoke of Harry. Who is he?'

Amy looked surprised, but replied without evasion:

'Her late fiancé, Harry Travers the skiing champion. Perhaps you've heard of him?'

Max gave a low whistle. 'That man!' he exclaimed. 'Yes, I have heard of him, and his reputation.'

Evelyn reached her room with her mind in a turmoil. She resented Max's interference, and yet she was grateful to him. The memories which the night had revived were overwhelming, but they had lost much of their pain. It could be that she was recovering from the shock of her loss, but it was quite unthinkable that she could ever put another man in Harry's place. Another man? What had suggested that? Had Max's attentions gone to her head, as if she were an excitable teenager returning from her first date? The man was personable, but she took no real interest in him, she had merely been stimulated by the music and movement, and of course the beastly vodka which Max had so unscrupulously administered. But that was the end of it. After tonight's fiasco he was unlikely to call again, which would be a relief, for he had troubled her, no doubt because she had been deprived not only of all amusement but of masculine society for so long.

Tomorrow everything would fall into its right perspective again, and this evening's experiences would have passed into limbo like an uneasy dream.

The following day was another one of sunshine. While Evelyn dressed, she viewed the long hours ahead which she and her aunt would try to fill with their little ploys, with dissatisfaction. It was a dull prospect and dimly she was aware that she was ripe for more active company, but it was unlikely that she would find it at the hotel.

As had been expected a new batch of visitors had arrived. Among them was a flighty-looking young woman with a staid husband, a Mrs. Lambert, with two unruly youngsters over whom she had little control. The other guests eyed them a little dubiously, foreseeing that Bobby and Jane would possibly prove a nuisance. There was also a young man with impudent brown eyes, who was regarding the assortment of middle-aged people who made up the bulk of the clientele with disfavour. As Evelyn stalked by his table to breakfast at her own, she heard him ask the waitress:

'And who is the Duchess?'

Inspired by some newly awakened spirit of coquetry, she turned in her seat and gave him a brilliant smile.

'I shouldn't encourage him,' Amy said disapprovingly.

'He looks cheeky.'

'Don't worry,' Evelyn returned, taking a roll from the pile in the basket on the table. 'I can keep him in his place.' She sniffed appreciatively at the coffee pot. 'I must say the coffee here is always excellent. And now what about those excursions?'

Amy was delighted by Evelyn's animation. Usually in the mornings she was unresponsive and withdrawn.

'It's too late to book for anything today,' she pointed out. 'Though we could go up to the Rosshutte in the funicular, but I've something laid on for tomorrow.'

'That sounds exciting.' Evelyn spoke indifferently, as she buttered her roll. She was not really very interested in excursions, but anything would be better than hanging around watching her aunt knit.

'Knowing how you dislike coaches, we're going by car.' Amy was talking very fast as if she feared protest. 'For a whole day, over the Brenner into Italy to see the Dolomites. I'm told the scenery is quite magnificent. I only hope the good weather holds up.'

Evelyn looked at her suspiciously. 'Whose car?'

'Well ... er ... actually Mr. Linden's. It seemed some arrangement of his fell through and he's got nothing to do tomorrow. I thought it was so nice of him to offer.'

'Oh, did you!' Evelyn repressed a faint stir of excitement. 'And you accepted for both of us?'

'But of course. I couldn't go without you. It's such an opportunity, dear, and I'm sure you'll enjoy it.'

'It seems to me it's accepting rather a lot from Mr. Linden,' Evelyn said doubtfully. 'We don't want to be under an obligation to him.'

'I don't think we should be. It's just a friendly gesture. It would be most ungracious to refuse.'

'I suppose you hatched this up after I'd gone to bed,'

40

Evelyn remarked. 'Why do you imagine he wants to be friendly?'

'Oh, he's just offering the hospitality of his country,' Amy said glibly. 'I gather your expedition last night wasn't very successful. He said he ought not to have taken you to such a crowded place, and he was sure some mountain air would do you good.'

'Very thoughtful of him,' Evelyn exclaimed scornfully, flushing a little. So that was how Max had accounted for their early return! Evidently he had not been put off by her odd behaviour, but she could hardly persuade herself that he felt the same attraction towards her that she had felt for him, not since she had become such a drab creature, and she had certainly not been encouraging. Not wholly ignorant of men, she knew that a man like Max, no longer in his first youth with his looks and charm, could not be without experience of women. Perhaps he was sated with accessible beauties and her aloofness presented a challenge to him. She was surprised that her aunt was so ready to accept favours from a stranger. Only yesterday she had questioned Max's respectability.

'I suppose Max ... Mr. Linden ... has presented his credentials?' she asked sarcastically. 'You no longer regard him as a possible menace?'

Amy looked embarrassed. 'I'm sure he's a very nice person,' she said defensively. 'He told me ... er ... quite a lot about his business ... a directorship of some sort. The only thing I find strange is that he's here alone. He doesn't seem to be attached, no female appendage in tow.'

'Perhaps he's been crossed in love,' Evelyn suggested. 'Or perhaps she died.'

A shadow crossed her face, and the old brooding look returned to her eyes. 'But men aren't like women,' she went on with a tinge of bitterness. 'They quickly console themselves.'

'It's more sensible than making oneself miserable and everyone else too,' Amy declared tartly.

Evelyn was faintly surprised. It was the first time that her aunt had ever reproached her, the first time that she had referred even obliquely to her loss.

'I'm afraid I must be an awful wet blanket,' she said apologetically. 'I don't know why you asked me to come with you.'

'Because I'm very fond of you,' Amy explained. 'I'd give anything to see you your old self again.'

'I'm afraid that's impossible, but I'll try to be more cheerful,' Evelyn promised, feeling a genuine compunction for her lack of responsiveness. 'And I'll go on this expedition to the Dolomites if you want to go, though I'm afraid Mr. Linden will soon find out that I'm incurably depressive, and will want to wash his hands of us.'

Amy said nothing, but she looked complacent.

In spite of the reluctance which she had shown when the idea was put to her, Evelyn began to look forward to the next day. It would be a change to get away from Seefeld and the confines of the pension. The new road over the Brenner Pass was an architectural marvel which she had been told everyone should see. She would not admit to herself that she very much wanted to see Max again.

They spent the morning sitting in the walled public garden with its view of the church across the road. Flower beds surrounded its paved walks, an artificially blue pond was in its centre. The traffic rumbled by along the narrow road that ran through the town.

Evelyn looked up at the narrow square-sided church

tower with its tall spire. It had been a monastery church, and behind it the Klosterbrau Hotel embodied part of the old monastery in its buildings. The courtyard belonging to it was one of the showplaces of the town, with its stone-arched cloisters and mural paintings upon the white-washed walls of the surrounding buildings, depicting scenes from history, especially the monastic history of the Order. Painting on the walls of houses was a common practice in the Tyrol.

If she had wanted to keep her lost love unviolated, she should have become a nun. In the ancient days, the convent had been the refuge of lovelorn women, but she was not especially devout, and though there were Anglican Orders, convents had always seemed to her to be essentially Catholic. Such self-immolation had not seemed necessary, since she had been so certain that she could never love again. Now she wished that she had erected an impenetrable barrier between herself ... and what? She was being quite absurd; there was an immense difference between being superficially drawn towards a personable man and falling in love. She had known Harry intimately for several months before they had discovered the state of their feelings, and she had only met Max twice.

Upon closer acquaintance, she might find that she disliked him. She certainly had resented his interference. The outer cover was alluring, almost devastatingly so, but she knew nothing of the man inside it. Tomorrow might well disillusion her.

'Time for lunch,' Amy announced, folding her knitting. 'You've been very thoughtful, dear.'

'I've quite a lot to think about,' Evelyn confessed. 'For once.' But though Amy looked at her inquiringly, she did not elucidate. Instead, she said:

'I think we've just time to buy some postcards. I really

43

must send some to Mother and Dad.'

Amy was delighted. She had been distressed by Evelyn's apparent indifference towards her parents.

The afternoon turned showery. Evelyn wrote on and dispatched her postcards, finding a short diversion in buying *briefmarken* from the post office, when she aired her slight knowledge of German. By dinner time she had almost got to the point of wishing Max would come and suggest some more dancing.

Coming into the lounge after the meal, she encountered the young man of the morning, sitting there alone with a glass of beer in front of him, looking disconsolate. As she appeared, he sprang to his feet, making her a mock bow.

'Good evening, Duchess.'

Hitherto Evelyn had more or less ignored her fellow guests. In her more receptive mood, she smiled at this one, guessing he was feeling lonely, and there was a flattering look of admiration in his brown eyes. Evelina Ravelli had always been gracious to her admirers.

'Come and sit down,' he said beguilingly. 'And talk to me. My sister who came with me has deserted me to go out with a man old enough to be her uncle and I'm all alone in a strange land among a crowd of foreigners.'

'Most of the people staying here are British,' Evelyn pointed out, sitting down beside him on the upholstered bench.

'British is the operative word. Most of those who came with us were Scots. One even addressed me as "wee mannie". I didn't know there were real people who talked like that.'

Astonished by this new development, Amy took herself to a distant corner, while Evelyn accepted a sherry from her new acquaintance, who told her that he was called

44

Jake Armstrong and this was his first trip abroad.

'The things they give you to eat!' he complained. 'They don't seem to have heard of bacon and eggs or fish and chips.'

'On a continental holiday you must expect to eat what the natives do,' Evelyn told him. 'That's what I like about this place, they don't try to give you English food.'

Hitherto she had not really noticed the food, but she recalled that that evening they had had fried veal with rice and apfelstrudel.

Jake made a face. 'So I'll have to put up with it. The beer's good anyway, even if it does cost the earth.'

The sister came in with her middle-aged escort and Evelyn was included in the quartet. Mary Armstrong was brown-eyed and brown-haired like her brother, but unlike him she was enthusiastic about everything Tyrolean. They were undemanding and easy to talk to and in their company Evelyn relaxed. Amy looked across at her and saw that she was laughing at some naïveté expressed by the Armstrong pair and she heaved a sigh of relief. Evelyn was at last beginning to react naturally to human companionship. Perhaps it would even be possible to persuade her to discard her magpie garments. She had used to look so well in colours.

The Armstrongs were only very ordinary young people, but they were young, and Evelyn needed to find her youth again. Max had given her a push along the road back to normality, and his action was bearing fruit. There was colour in the girl's cheeks and her dark eyes were sparkling. Amy wished he could have been there to witness the metamorphosis.

So, for that matter, did Evelyn.

However, next morning Evelyn suffered a sharp reaction against both Max and Jake. She was her aloof and unapproachable self again. Doubts and probings had given her a wakeful night, and Harry had come to her in her dreams, accusing her of desertion. She wished fervently that she had not agreed to go upon the expedition to the Brenner, but could see no way of avoiding it, unless she pleaded illness and that she scorned to do, convinced that Max would see through her ruse and despise her for it.

She was spared the Armstrongs' presence at breakfast, as they had left early upon an all-day excursion.

Amy noticed her pale cheeks and sombre eyes with dismay, but comforted herself by reflecting that Rome was not built in a day, and Evelyn was bound to take some backward steps.

They were both dressed for the outing. Evelyn in white trousers, white sandals and a white pullover, her hair as usual hanging in a long braid over one shoulder. Amy was conventionally clad in a blue two-piece, with a small-brimmed felt hat.

After the meal, they sat on the terrace waiting for Max to arrive. Evelyn was morose, her eyes fixed upon the distant summit of Hohe Munde, rising above the green slopes beyond the houses across the road. The rain had cleared and the sun shone brilliantly, promising good views of the mountains.

Jane and Bobby Lambert were playing on the grass and gravel below the steps, bouncing a ball. The ball shot over the low stone parapet into Evelyn's lap. Mechanically she picked it up and threw it back again, brushing the dust it had brought with it from her knees.

'*Danke schön, Fräulein*,' Bobby called. He came up to the parapet and peered up at her. He had a gamin face with an engaging grin. 'That's German, you know. Aren't I smart to have learned so much already?'

Evelyn made no response.

'Very clever,' Amy told him, wanting to shake her niece.

Bobby put his head on one side and perversely continued to try to attract Evelyn's attention.

'Do you know any German, miss?'

'He's speaking to you,' Amy prompted.

Evelyn came out of her dreary trance and stared blankly at the mischievous face smiling up at her.

'I threw your ball back,' she said coldly.

'I asked if you knew any German, miss. I know lots.'

'Do you? How nice,' Evelyn returned flatly.

Bobby gave it up. Surreptitiously, he put out his tongue at her.

Amy saw the gesture, but did not reprimand him, in fact she sympathized. Sometimes she despaired of her niece.

Evelyn could not have explained why she had snubbed the child. She liked children, and she and Harry had planned to have a family. That was partly why she had been prepared to give up her musical triumphs. Something in that impish face had hurt her. She had dreamed of a son with just such a look. Now she would never have a son.

Both children scattered as Max's car swung into the open space before the hotel.

He sprang out and ran lightly up the steps. At night, in his conventional clothes, he had looked a distinguished man of the world. This morning, in light sweater and slacks, he looked much younger, almost boyish.

'Grüss Gott, ladies!' he greeted them gaily.

'Grüss Gott, Grüss Gott!' chanted Bobby from below. 'That's a new one.'

Max turned and surveyed him.

'Where does that come from?' he asked, smiling.

'It's staying here,' Evelyn told him, 'and it's studying the language.'

'Very admirable,' Max declared, and addressed the gamin in his own tongue.

'That's too hard for me,' Bobby said said sadly.

'Try,' Max coaxed. '*Wie geht es ihnen* – that means, how are you.'

Bobby repeated the syllables almost recognizably.

'Fine, you have the makings of a linguist,' Max told him solemnly.

Bobby looked smug. 'Was I good?'

'Very good – *sehr gut*.'

'Then if I was *gut*, you wouldn't by any chance give me the price of an ice lolly?' Bobby asked insinuatingly. 'Jane and me, we like ice lollies and they sell them even in Austria, at a shop round the corner.'

'You seem to have learnt your way about,' Max said genially. He took out his pocketbook and extricated a twenty-schilling note. 'I think that should cover your requirements.'

Bobby, who had not expected his gambit to be so successful, accepted it with awe.

'Thank you,' he said, 'I mean *danke schön*. Jane ...' turning to his sister who had been watching the scene with interest. 'Say *danke schön*.'

'Shan't,' Jane returned. 'I'm English.' She smiled engagingly at Max. 'Thank you very much.'

'Jane doesn't want to be a lin ... what you said,' Bobby explained, 'that's because she's a girl, girls is silly.'

'You're the silly,' Jane retorted, 'wanting to work on holiday. But what about those lollies?'

Bobby hesitated, glancing at Max. 'Would you like one too?' he asked. 'I expect this'll buy more than two.'

Max declined decidedly and the two children ran off happily.

Evelyn had watched this little scene with critical eyes. Who, she wondered, was he trying to impress?

'You seem fond of children,' she remarked.

'As a matter of fact, I am. Aren't you?'

'Not particularly,' she said untruthfully, and met his eyes challengingly. 'Because I'm a woman, it doesn't mean that I automatically must have maternal instincts. My life is ... was ... filled with quite different interests.'

'Such as?' he prompted gently.

She turned her head away. Those interests were finished.

'Oh, nothing exciting,' she said drearily. Instinctively she pushed her left hand into her trouser pocket.

Max regarded her in silence with a slight frown. Then he turned away.

'Shall we be off?' he inquired. 'We are lucky in our weather. You have your passports with you?'

'I always carry mine,' Amy said, while Evelyn asked: 'Why do we need them?'

'We shall be crossing into Italy.'

Italy! In spite of herself, Evelyn's interest quickened. What visions of blue-skied magic the word conjured up. Even though they were only travelling into the northern part of it. She sprang up almost eagerly and ran down the steps, while Max gave a hand to her aunt.

CHAPTER THREE

EVELYN was a competent driver, but her car had been sold after the accident, as her father had not wished her to drive alone, fearing that she might do herself some mischief. She had been in other cars since, the vehicles were too much a part of modern living to be able to avoid them, though she had at first shrunk from travelling in one. But her initial nervousness had long since worn off, and she was frankly appreciative of the machine which Max was driving. It ran smoothly, the engine was quiet but powerful, and the interior spacious. She had insisted that Amy went in front, while she went in the back, and her aunt's small figure looked lost in the big bucket seat.

Max drove through the shallow green bowl which enclosed the red-roofed houses of Reith, and from thence over the Zirlerberg, through a wooded gorge with peaks appearing on each side, and then the steep descent into the Innthal, and along the valley road into Innsbruck, sprawling across the Inn River under the frowning cliffs of the Nordkette.

'We must come here another day,' Amy remarked. 'I believe there are good shops.'

'So there are,' Max corroborated. 'I have friends in the town with whom I often lunch. Let me know when you want to go and I will run you in.'

'You're very kind,' Amy murmured, and Evelyn said coolly:

'We needn't trouble you. We can always go by train.'

'But if I am going in anyway, you would find the car

more comfortable,' he insisted.

Evelyn let the subject drop. They were not going to Innsbruck today, but much further afield. By the time evening came Max might well have decided they were far too dull to wish to repeat his offer.

The wide autobahn out of Innsbruck snaked up to the pass in graceful curves, crossing the valleys by long bridges.

The first, the Bergisel, passed near the hill where Andreas Hofer had fought his great battle for Tyrolean freedom, and where his statue stands in the park of that name. Then, after passing through a tunnel, it ascended smoothly, while Innsbruck fell behind them and the scenery increased in grandeur at every bend. Far below ran the old road and the railway, both passing under the Europa Bridge, which, as Max remarked, could only be really admired from beneath it, not while crossing it. They were halted at the tollgate, but that was their only stop. The railway, now on their left hand, went through Matrei and Steinach, towns sheltered deep in the valley, upon the roofs of which travellers along the autobahn could look down upon from the steep embankment. Valleys pierced the hills upon either side, green ravines between the soaring mountains, the most noticeable one being that of St. Jodok, where the railway tunnelled through a pine-clad hill and the green grass studded with hamlets, each with its conspicuous church tower, wound away between the tree-covered hills to a vista of snow-streaked peaks. The road was a superb piece of engineering, crossing wide gorges and rising so gradually that the steep ascent was unnoticeable.

'It would have made the Romans stare,' Max remarked with satisfaction, 'superb builders though they were. This has always been the main route from Germany to Italy even in those distant days.'

Finally they reached the frontier between Italy and Austria, and presented their passports, which received only a cursory glance from the Austrian officials, but the swarthy Italians upon the further side gave them closer attention, favouring Evelyn with long appraising stares.

Max moved impatiently in his seat. 'Impertinent devils,' he muttered as they drove off.

'They were only doing their duty,' Evelyn said sweetly.

'Exceeding it.'

On the further side the autobahn soon ceased, though work upon furthering it was visible parallel with their descent. Ultimately it was planned to carry it to Rome, but it looked a long way off completion. As it was early in the year there was not a great deal of traffic, although they had met several long buses toiling up either side of the pass carrying their loads of sightseers.

Throughout the journey, Max had displayed a genuine pride and pleasure in showing his passengers the engineering marvel of the bridge and its accompanying scenic grandeur. Evelyn decided that his purpose in bringing them was simply to win their admiration for his country and his countrymen's handiwork. This innocent pride of his was oddly endearing, rather like that of a small boy exhibiting a magnificent clockwork toy. It was surprising that someone apparently so sophisticated could be so naïve about it.

The country on the further side was very similar to that through which they had already travelled, but as they progressed further south, Max pointed out little terraced vineyards and gardens built into the hillsides, and as the mountains decreased in height the air seemed warmer.

Officially they were in Italy, though the towns of that lost province, which had once been part of Austria, still defiantly used their old names in preference to their newer Italian ones.

This was emphasized at Sterzing, which the Italians called Vipiteno. This was an old town, still Austrian in character, with stone-arched arcades along its main street. Here Max suggested stopping for coffee.

Amy had been very silent during the latter part of the journey. Now, as Max handed her out of the car, Evelyn noticed that she was looking very pale. It was so warm that they were able to sit outside the café, though they were practically on the street. Amy had expressed a need for air. Now she confessed that she was either car-sick or affected by the high altitude at the top of the pass.

'I suppose we'd better go back,' Eve said a little wistfully. She had enjoyed the journey over the pass and was eager to see the Dolomites. The wonderful scenery had taken her right out of her depression and preoccupations. Here, in this little Italian town, she felt like a child playing truant from school. The trip had taken on a holiday atmosphere. The old problems awaited her upon her return, but temporarily among a welter of new impressions, she was freed from her obsessions.

Amy would not hear of that. For one thing, she did not feel equal to re-crossing the pass until she had had time to recuperate. She pointed out that Max's return route would include Vitipeno, and she could stay there until they came back. She would enjoy exploring it, and she would get herself some lunch. She would never forgive herself if she allowed herself to spoil their day.

'I had intended to go up into the mountains,' Max said, 'and the Sella Pass is higher than the Brenner, but we could of course go somewhere else. Merano or Brixen are

53

not far.'

Amy had seen the flash of disappointment cross Evelyn's face, and knew Max wanted to show the mountains to her. She continued to insist that she preferred to remain where she was.

'I'll get some travel sickness pills from the chemist ... Oh, yes, Max, I know enough German not to need your help, and most of the shop assistants speak some English. I was stupid not to think of them before. I'd much rather stay quietly here on my own, if you don't mind.'

She had called him Max quite naturally, Evelyn noticed, she had definitely accepted him.

After a little more persuasion they agreed to fall in with Amy's plan and eventually set off together. It was not until she was seated beside him that Evelyn realized that she would be completely alone with Max for the next few hours and almost regretted her decision. But a new spirit of adventure was coming to birth within her, and she recklessly decided that she did not care what happened.

'Where are we going?' she asked.

'Up to the Karer Pass. It is the entrance to the Dolomites, which cover a vast area, and of course we can only touch the fringe of it. On the Karer we shall have the Rosengarten on one side and the Latemar on the other, and there is a hotel where I can give you lunch.'

'You're being very good to me,' she said impulsively.

Seeing the change in her, he caught a glimpse of the girl which she once had been. He said simply:

'I hope to give you pleasure.'

'But why?' she asked curiously. 'Why do you want to please me? I haven't been exactly charming to you!'

He smiled enigmatically. 'Perhaps I will tell you that some day.'

'You're being very mysterious!'

He shrugged his shoulders. 'Let the whys and where-fores take care of themselves. Today we have no past and no future. We shall enjoy the sunshine and this lovely world, shall we not? Please to accept that and live for the moment.'

That she was quite ready to do. Her past was left behind, even Amy was not there to remind her of it. The future was nebulous and at that moment she felt carefree and even happy. She had not believed she could ever feel happy again.

Their way continued down the sunny valley. Max pointed out to her the acres of wire netting spread over the rocks above the road to prevent the shale bleeding into it.

'There can be avalanches of stones besides snow,' he remarked.

Then he turned off the main highway to travel up a narrow winding gorge, with a river running many feet below the road, and densely wooded slopes rising on either side. At one point a castle stood on a spur, without any visible approach.

'Truly Gothic,' Max remarked as he drew her attention to it. 'How would you like to be shut up up there?'

'A bit grim, but at least there would be a marvellous view.'

'For those who have eyes to see it. Some of us shut ourselves up in equally inaccessible places, and refuse to look at the view.'

Suspecting a double meaning, Evelyn ignored this remark, turning her attention to the river down below where some people were fishing.

'Trout?' she asked.

'I expect so. Perhaps we shall get some for lunch.'

Eventually the road steepened sharply, the trees fell away, and the first peaks of the Dolomites came into view, a serrated ridge, looking grey and formidable.

'The Latemar,' Max told her.

Farther on the Rosengarten on the other side became visible. The magnesium in the rocks caused them to glow red in the sunset, he told her, hence their name, the Rose garden, but in the clear midday light they were only faintly pink. Their upper portions were sheer steep rock, and looked deceptively near in the clear air. The Karer Pass ran between the two ridges, and here was an hotel, a souvenir shop and other buildings.

'This is where we will lunch,' Max announced, and turned into the car park.

The air was as exhilarating as wine. Before them between the massive peaks on either hand, other more distant mountains raised snow-streaked heads into a cloudless blue sky. They were lucky in their day, there was no mist to obscure the view.

Evelyn felt that she had stepped into another world. She was entranced by the magnificent scenery on either side, invigorated by the pine-scented air. They talked desultorily over their meal, which did include trout, about the country, and its customs, and then Max mentioned the winter sports, which, together with rock-climbing, were so much a feature of it. He was, he said, very keen on skiing. That recalled Harry, and a shadow crossed Evelyn's face; she did not want to think of Harry today. Max noticed it, and quickly changed the subject. Throughout the meal he was watching the girl, noticing the improvement in her looks, the eager light in her eyes, the vivacity with which she questioned him. She was beautiful when she was animated, like a classical statue endowed with life, but only the surface was touched as yet. All too easily she could slip back into her former painful brooding, as was apparent when he had mentioned skiing.

The meal concluded with the excellent coffee which was always obtainable in that part of the world, and he proposed a walk to stretch their legs.

Evelyn acquiesced with alacrity, and they crossed the road to follow a slightly muddy path leading into a field. This was completely covered with small white crocuses growing so close together that it was impossible to avoid treading upon them. Evelyn exclaimed with delight; she had never seen wild crocuses nor imagined such profusion. Further on were scattered trees, and a mountain stream babbled gaily by. There were still patches of snow in places, and where the ground rose towards the mountains, there was a snow field.

They crossed the little stream at its narrowest point, Evelyn scorning Max's outstretched hand, and jumping it easily. Max turned downhill, and the trees thickened, pine and larch, the latter fresh with new green foliage. They were screened from any other travellers, and beneath them they could glimpse the houses in the Fassa valley, far, far below.

'I'll never forget this!' Evelyn cried enthusiastically. 'Thank you, thank you, for bringing me.'

'It is my pleasure, Eve,' he told her gravely, 'and it is a still greater pleasure to me to see the ghosts driven away.'

She stopped and looked at him uncertainly.

'Are they so terrible those ghosts?' he asked. 'Can't they be exorcized for ever?'

The animation died from her face and the old haunted expression crept into her eyes.

'I don't know what you mean,' she said coldly. 'I can't

forget my memories, nor do I want to.'

But why must he remind her now, when for a little while she had forgotten? It was tactless of him, she thought resentfully, but then he had no inkling of how bitter they were.

'That is your trouble,' he told her gravely. 'You deliberately try to keep them alive. You should let the past die.'

'Never!' she cried passionately. 'And what do you know of my past anyway?'

He smiled quizzically. 'You yourself admitted on that first day that you had loved and lost.'

'I don't remember what I said. I was upset, and I've asked you before to forget that incident.'

'You must do some forgetting also. You will love again, Eve. At twenty-five, you cannot close the doors on love.'

He had come very close to her, an intent look in his eyes. She turned her own gaze across the distant valley, intensely aware of the strong, masculine body so near her own. Excitement stirred her pulses, and she tried desperately to quell it.

'Perhaps this will help you to forget,' he said coolly.

She had been a fool to imagine he would let the day pass without making some sort of amorous advance. The opportunity was too good to miss; subconsciously she had been expecting something of the kind ever since she had encountered him. It was only surprising that he had not made more use of her weakness upon the night of the dance. That was why she had tried to snub him. What she was totally unprepared for was her own response. Her starved senses awoke in rapturous acceptance, her arms crept round his neck, her body melted into his. He held her closely and his kisses were expert. Deliberately he was trying to rouse her. She clung to him, her lips parting under his, while ecstasy flooded her being. She closed her eyes, and as on that other night, she had the illusion that Harry had returned to her.

Abruptly he released her.

'You're cheating,' he said angrily.

Evelyn opened her eyes to the realization that this man was not her dead love, but almost a stranger who had taken an unpardonable liberty. Yet her heart continued to beat wildly and she could not meet the flame in his eyes.

'You shouldn't have done that,' she said fiercely. 'I suppose because I made a fool of myself the other night, you think you needn't respect me.'

'Respect?' he asked mockingly. 'What a word!' Then he smiled. 'I was unmannerly to take you out and not to kiss you,' he quoted.

She recognized Shakespeare, but it did little to appease her.

'So it's part of the routine when you take a girl out,' she said, her voice shaking. Colour rose to her pale cheeks, as anger flamed in her. 'It's a part I could dispense with.'

He laughed triumphantly. 'I have made you feel, even if you did have to pretend I was another man.'

She was astonished by his perception, and incoherently she tried to excuse herself.

'No one has kissed me since … it was an instinctive reaction. I … I'm only human.'

'Then act like a human woman instead of an automaton,' he told her. 'Your reaction was perfectly normal. What you need is to be kissed very thoroughly until you have rid yourself of your absurd obsessions.'

He made a movement towards her as if he intended to carry out his prescription, and Evelyn backed nervously away from him. She did not know what would happen if he did, and it occurred to her in a flash of illumination that she had not, after all, reacted to Harry's memory, but to Max himself.

Striving to regain her normal calm, she said icily:

'I should be obliged if you would take me back to my aunt at once.'

'We have reached the point of no return,' he told her significantly, and she wondered wildly what he meant, but he went on to explain that it would be no shorter to go back than to continue their planned route.

'Meanwhile we are alone on top of a mountain pass,' he said suggestively, and took a step towards her. She threw a glance behind her, feeling trapped, and saw with relief that there were other people coming through the trees.

'We aren't,' she told him, 'and if you're going to continue to be so . . . so objectionable, I'll beg a lift . . .'

'And find yourself out of the frying pan into the fire. You are too decorative to beg lifts from strangers without risk. In fact, Eve, when you are roused you are too uncomfortably alluring.'

'Am I supposed to say thank you for a compliment?' she asked scornfully. 'Really, Mr. Linden . . .!'

'My name is Max,' he interrupted.

'I know that, but I prefer to call you Mr. Linden. You deliberately tried to rouse me, didn't you? What was your object?'

'It is obvious, *nicht wahr?*'

'How?'

'Do you think I like to see a young and lovely girl persisting in burying herself in the ashes of her past? Not only is it unnatural, but it is a shocking waste.'

'When she might be bestowing her favours upon creeps

like you!' Evelyn flung at him. 'I call that a waste.' And immediately regretted the word which she had used. Max was not a creep, but she doubted if he understood the expression.

Speaking more gently, she continued, 'I'm faithful, Ma ... Mr. Linden, to my dead. And he is dead, poor Harry.'

'But he has been dead for two years now,' Max exploded, betraying that he knew more of her history than she had told him. Fleetingly she wondered from whence he had obtained his information. It must have been Amy.

'*Du liebe Gott*,' he went on angrily, 'you are not even his widow, and if he were anything of a man, he would want you to find happiness again.'

'You just don't understand,' she said loftily. 'Ours was the love of a lifetime. Now I'm going back to the hotel and I'll telephone for a car to take me back to Sterzing. Good-bye, Mr. Linden.'

How Amy and herself were to be conveyed back over the Brenner, she did not pause to consider. Vaguely she recalled that there were trains. She was determined to get away from Max as quickly as possible.

She had only taken a few steps when a couple of long strides brought him up beside her, and he laid a detaining hand upon her arm. She swung round to face him, while a faint excitement quivered along her nerves to find him so close to her again. To her horror, she had to resist an urge to throw herself into his arms.

'Do not be foolish, *liebchen*,' he said gently. 'The cost of such transport would be prohibitive, and you could not condemn your poor aunt to a long rail journey back to Seefeld. We will call a truce until you are safe under her wing again. I would not take advantage of your helplessness, you know, and I have achieved enough for one day.'

This remark struck her as being ambiguous, but she was relieved. She doubted very much if she could have made herself understood over the telephone and as he had pointed out the expense of hiring a car would have been hideously great if she had.

'You promise to behave?' she asked doubtfully.

He released his hold, clicked his heels together and bowed to her.

'I swear to you my behaviour will be impeccable.' But mischief still lurked in his eyes.

'You won't touch me?' She knew now that contact with him could be dangerous.

'I vow I will not – whatever the provocation.'

'I hope you're a man of your word.' She was disdainful.

He looked pained. 'You are cruel to doubt me.'

'Oh, very well.' She turned away from him, but in her agitation she did not heed where she was treading. She wanted to reach the car by the quickest route, but they were far below the place where they had crossed the stream, and lower down, encountering some obstacle, it had overflowed and the surrounding terrain was swampy. Evelyn blundered into it without realizing the peril to her footgear. She sank ankle deep in mud and both sandals and trouser bottoms were covered in it when she reached the shelving ground on the farther side.

Max had found a narrower crossing which he had leaped effortlessly, and he stood watching her floundering progress with an inscrutable expression on his face, and his hands thrust into his trouser pockets.

Her face scarlet with mortification, Eve scrambled up the bank to stand beside him, aware that her feet were soaking.

'You should look where you are going,' he remarked calmly. 'Did it escape your notice that the stream narrows again a few yards farther down?'

She knew he was perfectly well aware that her agitation had made her careless.

'You could have warned me.' Her eyes flashed with rage. He had neither called out nor offered to help her.

'I had no chance to stay your impetuous progress until it was too late,' he pointed out with a mocking glint in his eyes. 'I would have willing offered you a helping hand, or even have lifted you across, but that would have meant breaking my promise, because I *am* a man of my word, Eve, and I had no option except to restrain my chivalrous impulses and allow you to get out of the morass in your own way.'

His tone implied a deeper meaning than the mere negotiation of a mountain stream, but she was too angry to notice it.

'Brute!' she exclaimed, turning away.

'Now, Eve, be fair.'

'All right, you win.' Inadequately she tried to wipe off the worst of the mud from her sandals on the short grass, aware of appearing ludicrous. A dramatic situation had ended in bathos, and all because she had not had the sense to pick her way.

'I am afraid that will not do much good,' he observed, watching her efforts with ill-concealed amusement, which infuriated her even more. 'Let us go to the car, where you can take them off. You will not have to do any more walking.'

'I should hope not!' she exclaimed vehemently, and squelched her way towards where the car was parked. Once, as she stumbled, he put out his hand to help her, but instantly drew it back. She saw the movement and it did nothing to pacify her. Max was making a mockery of the promise which she had exacted from him. It was his method of getting his own back.

When she was installed in the car, he handed her a duster.

'You can wipe the worst off with that,' he told her.

While she was thus employed he went to open the boot and came back dangling a pair of blue sandals.

'Perhaps these will fit you,' he suggested. 'You can wear them while yours dry.'

Tactfully he withdrew while she effected the change. The sandals were dainty objects, obviously a woman's and actually a size too small for her, but as they were open-toed, she could get her feet into them.

Max had offered no explanation for the presence of a pair of very feminine sandals in the boot of his car. She doubted if he would do so. Their appearance raised speculations. Were they the residue of some earlier expedition with another girl? Did Max make a practice of taking young women up into the mountains and kissing them to test their reactions? She found the supposition far from agreeable. Her face burned as she bent over her task – she had made an utter idiot of herself. If only she had been able to maintain her usual dignified aloofness, and if in the face of it he had still dared to make a pass at her, slapped his face. What could he think of the way in which she had responded to him? But then he had expected it. He had banked upon releasing the repressions of the past years with his ardour. She remembered his look of triumph at his success and her indignation positively seethed. He was a vain, hateful creature and Amy should have known better than to have encouraged him. She must have told him about Harry's demise, and

Evelyn fervently hoped that was all, but she was sure Amy would not have revealed whom she had been. That, she was determined Max should never know. Evelina Ravelli kissed under a fir tree and abandoned in a bog! That was too humiliating.

She wiped the worst of the mud off her trouser legs, and hoped that when it had dried she could brush off some more, but they were hopelessly stained. She wore no stockings and her feet and ankles looked white, even frail, in the borrowed sandals. At least they were nicely shaped, she thought with faint satisfaction, for Max was sure to notice them.

Sure enough he did, and his glance lingered on them as he slid into his seat beside her.

'That looks better,' he remarked.

'Whom do the sandals belong to?' she asked.

'To tell you the truth I do not know. I ferry various friends about and I remembered noticing they had been forgotten, but by whom and why . . .' he shrugged.

'Girl-friends?' she asked disdainfully, feeling sure that he was lying.

He shot her an impish glance as he let in the clutch.

'Obviously those sandals belong to a girl.'

'Obviously,' she agreed icily. She was about to inquire further about his lady friends, but checked herself in time. They were no concern of hers, and he might even imagine that she was jealous. She smiled at the mere notion.

The car slid over the summit of the pass and began the winding descent upon the farther side. Though seemingly intent upon his driving, Max had seen that smile.

'What is amusing you, Eve?'

'My thoughts, and I never said you could use my name.'

'It is usual, *nicht wahr,* among the youth of today, or do you consider I am no longer young?'

She had not tried to place his age. Fair men often looked more youthful than they were, but Max was definitely not a boy.

'You can't be very young if you can hold a position which justifies a car like this one,' she reasoned, mentally assessing the cost of running the big Mercedes, and hoping he would tell her what he did.

'An astute piece of deduction, but fallible,' he told her, 'I might in addition to my salary have private means, or I might have stolen it.'

'Is that another of your hobbies?' she asked idly, disappointed by the failure of her ruse.

'What?'

'Stealing cars,' she said maliciously.

'I have not tried it, but what is my other hobby?'

'Experimenting with girls.'

He laughed. 'So you think this afternoon's episode was an experiment?'

'Wasn't it?'

'*Ach,* no,' he denied firmly.

'Then how else would you describe your conduct?'

'Provocative, aren't you? To explain fully I would need both my hands to demonstrate and perhaps you have not noticed that this road requires not only my hands, but all my skill and concentration. Suppose you give your attention to the scenery intead of trying to interrogate me. It is what we have come to see.'

Feeling rebuked and justly, she turned to look out of the window. The road was descending steeply into the Fassa valley, the Rosengarten towering above them on their left, a vista of mountains over on the right. An Italianate village nestled in the valley, which was neither

Italian nor Austrian, speaking a Romance language which derived from Latin.

'You can see Marmola, too, in the distance,' Max told her. 'That is the highest peak in the Dolomites. After traversing the valley, we shall ascend the Sella, which is over seven thousand feet up, and the road to it has twenty-seven hairpin bends. You will see the famous rock face on the Rosengarten which only ace climbers are allowed to try to scale. We are in fact circling that range of mountains.'

When they came to the rock face, she saw it was an enormous block of perpendicular ochre-coloured rock without apparent hand or foot hold. How vast it was was emphasized when they were able to discern a line of climbers in action. They looked like flies.

The Sella Pass was still deep in snow and when they reached the summit, Evelyn was amused to see the occupants of a touring coach had descended from their vehicle to enjoy a snowball battle. The air was crystal clear and her ears tingled with the high altitude.

Max pointed out the ski-runs with their accompanying chair-lifts still deep in snow. Evelyn looked at them curiously, for it was among such scenes that Harry had spent much of his life. The ski-runs in Austria, where he had taken part in the Winter Olympics, must have presented a similar appearance to these. Oddly enough, Harry had always discouraged her from making any attempt to ski herself, and his world of sport was as alien to her as her musical one was to him.

The snow disappeared as they started to descend, while Max pointed out objects of interest with the conscientiousness of a good courier. Gradually Evelyn's resentment against him died away, but try as she would to fix her mind upon mountain ppeaks, deep valleys and picturesque villages, she became more and more aware of the man sitting so close beside her, his strong fingers manipulating the big car so skilfully, his lean brown face, his crop of thick fair hair, which when the sunlight touched it gleamed with gold, his long, tawny eyelashes and the firm line of his jaw. He was more than just good-looking, with a subtle air of distinction, which suggested that he was used to command. Who was he, and what did he do? He had been reticent about himself and had evaded her hints, but she did not want to go too deeply into personal revelations, since she did not mean to make any about herself.

Sitting there beside him amid all that magnificent scenery, he seemed oddly familiar, as if she had known him, not for mere days, but for years. She seemed to be drawn to him by some empathy which had made her ready to forgive his outrageous behaviour on the Karer. The fact that they were two little specks in a vast region of rocks, forests and empty air might have something to do with it. The only real friendships she had ever formed, except her love for Harry, which came into a different category, were with musicians, music being their common bond, but as far as she knew, music meant nothing to Max, nor could she think of anything else which would account for the mysterious link which seemed to exist between them.

'You are very quiet,' he observed. 'Of what are you thinking?'

'That I don't know anything about you,' she answered candidly. 'I don't even know if you're married.'

He threw her a quick glance of reproach.

'Do you think I am the kind of man who leaves his wife behind when he goes on holiday?'

'How should I know what to think? But if you've no

wife, perhaps you are engaged?'

'I see that you are a true woman, interested only in matters of the heart. No, Eve, I am not affianced, but I hope that one day, with a little luck, I shall be.'

This information was unpalatable to Evelyn, she supposed because a man always became less interesting when he was attached. Impulsively she exclaimed:

'She must be hard to please if she can't make up her mind to accept you.'

'Thank you, that is the first really nice thing that you have said to me. You seem to have changed your opinion of me since we left the Karer.'

'You annoyed me, but I didn't behave very well either,' she admitted honestly. 'After all, men will be men.'

'Now what I wonder do you mean by that?'

'That I'm willing to forget it happened, and I hope you will also.'

'I have no wish to forget it,' he said quietly. 'It will become a treasured memory.'

Along with many similar ones, no doubt, she thought wryly. Perhaps he collected them. Aloud she said:

'Please, don't be flowery. We were talking about your fiancée.'

'But I told you I am not engaged.'

'Your intended then. I suppose you're in love with her?'

'*Ach*, what an inquisitive little lady you are! Love, you know, takes many forms. If I were to say I esteem and admire her, that she arouses my protective instincts, and I ask no better than to serve her all my life, would you call that love?'

It seemed a little cold to Evelyn. Her own romance had been much more tempestuous. There had been so much of young passion in it, a need for contact, the breathless rapture of shared kisses. Harry had never been protective that she could recall, he had been too demanding. She supposed that he had been prepared to shield and serve her, though she had been unaware of a need for either action. She had envisaged a long duet at an increasing tempo, an idyllic rhapsody ... Rhapsody – music – her music had gone too.

Becoming aware that Max seemed to be expecting a rejoinder, she said doubtfully:

'Yes, I suppose so, but as you say, there are many ways of loving.'

'And the one I have depicted is not exciting enough for you?' he queried, with a quizzical glance. 'There would be fire, also, but banked at first. I think at the moment my beloved is more in need of reassurance and cherishing.'

She must be a stupid, vapid doll, Evelyn thought contemptuously, if that was all she expected from her lover. But she was stung by Max's words. He had made no attempt to reassure or cherish herself, kissing her to amuse himself with her reaction and allowing her to muddy herself in the stream.

'Always providing you can control yourself,' she said nastily, and had the satisfaction of seeing his jaw tighten as her thrust went home.

Then he laughed. 'As you so aptly remarked, men will be men. Nevertheless I hope I shall be able to treat my bride with consideration and care.'

'Which if she's a real woman she won't appreciate in the least,' Evelyn retorted tartly.

'So that was not what you wanted?'

'Oh, please,' Evelyn cried with a stab of anguish. 'I wasn't aware of wanting anything. Our love was a perfect thing.'

'*Ach*, but I am clumsy!' he exclaimed contritely. 'I

brought you out to forget the bad memories, and now I have recalled them.'

'They aren't bad,' she told him fiercely. 'They're wonderful. They're all I have left.'

She covered her face with her hands. The car stopped. They had left the tortuous mountain road and turned into a carriageway. Max had pulled into a lay-by and come to a halt. Removing her hands, she looked at him a little apprehensively. He had turned in his seat and was regarding her compassionately.

'You have been more fortunate than you know to have such a memory to look back upon and that it ended without disillusion. But it is ended, Eve. Now you must look forward and not back, even if . . .' he checked himself.

Here we go again, Evelyn thought; why can't he leave the subject alone? She said suspiciously:

'Even if . . . what?' Then as he did not reply, she asked sharply, 'What did Aunt Amy tell you about me? She did tell you something, didn't she?'

'She did not tell me anything that I did not know,' he said earnestly, 'except your fiancé's name.' His face became a little grim. 'Travers' name was well known in the Tyrol. I had heard of his death.'

'And that was all?' Evelyn insisted.

'I do not tell lies, Eve.' He looked at her penetratingly. 'Is there something else, which you do not wish to be revealed?'

'Plenty,' she returned promptly, trying to speak lightly. 'Every woman has her little secrets.' But she could not meet his keen gaze. 'It must have been fun pulling me to pieces,' she went on scornfully, 'and you would have an ally in Aunt Amy. She thinks I've hugged my sorrow too long. Perhaps you think it's wrong to grieve?'

'For real grief I have the greatest respect, but you have

made yours into a cult and yourself into its high priestess. It has become an act, and I doubt if it is still genuine.'

He had angered her before, but now this plain speaking swept her into a blaze of fury.

'How dare you . . . how dare you!' she gasped, her eyes flashing. 'That's an abominable thing to say. I hate you! I loathe you!' She clenched her hands as if she would strike him. She was all the more incensed because she had a dreadful suspicion that there was truth in his words.

He bowed his head before her wrath and said quietly:

'I would dare even more to strip the veils from your eyes.'

'But what's it got to do with you?'

'That I will tell you when you are once more a real woman.'

That needled her even more.

'You're assuming that our acquaintance is going to continue,' she told him through quivering lips. 'I promise you that once we get back to Seefeld, I'll never speak to you again!'

He leaned back in his seat, regarding her through half-closed eyes, which masked his thoughts.

'You are quite magnificent when you're in a rage, Eve,' he said coolly. 'When were you last in such a passion?'

Sheer astonishment checked her fury.

'Why . . . I don't know . . . ages ago. Nobody has said anything to make me angry.'

'A pity,' he observed. 'Anger can act as an emotional release.'

'Did you . . . did you deliberately provoke me?' she demanded.

'Perhaps.'

'Really, Mr. Linden, I can't think of any epithet bad

enough to describe you,' she said savagely. 'First you kiss me, then you set out to insult me ... is psychology another of your hobbies?'

'I am not particularly interested in it, except in yours. Admit it, Eve, you have been more alive today than ... well, for a very long time.'

She had. She had run through a whole gamut of emotions which she had not expected to feel again. He had shattered the enshrouding wall of her apathy, but she was not going to thank him for doing it, his methods were too brutal.

'So you've been playing upon my feelings like a piano ...' she began heatedly, and stopped abruptly and turned her head away. Piano, the instrument which she had loved so dearly that she could not bear to think of it, nor even to speak its name. Max had taken her so far out of herself and her taboos that she had uttered it naturally, without thinking. What was he doing to her? Was nothing sacred to him? But he did not know what the piano had meant to her.

She turned back to him, her face a stony mask, her eyes glittering.

'I would be much obliged, Mr. Linden, if you would not say any more and would kindly drive me back to join my aunt as quickly as possisble.'

Max started the car in silence. He did not speak again until they had reached Sterzing. His face was no less stony than that of the girl beside him.

CHAPTER FOUR

EVELYN woke next morning with a curiously blank feeling, for which she could not at first account, and when a possible explanation presented itself, she rejected it with scorn. Taking her at her word, Max had not suggested a further meeting.

Fortified by her pills, Amy had suffered no ill effects from the return journey across the Brenner. She had asked interested questions about their trip into the mountains, and Evelyn had given her enthusiastic descriptions, sitting beside her in the rear seat the better to do so. But throughout she had been more than a little conscious of the man in front of her. He had made occasional interpolations when Evelyn had been unable to remember a name or a height in feet, but for most of the journey seemed to have withdrawn into his thoughts. She had already spoken of the stream in the crocus field to account for the mishap to her trousers, and made no further reference to it, though what had happened there was uppermost in her mind. Amy was too astute not to sense tension between her companions and she watched them both a little anxiously.

Arrived back in Seefeld, Max had brought up the matter of their proposed visit to Innsbruck, suggesting, with a satirical eye upon Evelyn, that as he was going there on the morrow, he could accommodate them with transport. But to her relief, Amy had prescribed a rest day after their long expedition, adding that when they did go, she was sure he would understand if she preferred to travel by train. He had agreed without demur, and taken his leave of them, almost, Evelyn thought, with thankfulness.

The long drive back through the mellow evening light, had done much to tranquillize her outraged emotions. Max had been infuriating, but possibly he meant well, and she had not been very adroit in her handling of him. At least she had repaid him for his entertainment by putting on a nice little firework display for him, she thought dourly. He could not complain of being bored with her company. But enough was enough. She would take good care that she was never alone with him again. Not that there seemed much chance of that. He had had his fun and they had parted with cool politeness, and that was that, except for this blankness upon awakening.

Resolutely Evelyn pushed Max out of her mind and turned to the photograph of Harry which always stood beside her bed. Before it was a little pot containing wild flowers, principally blue gentians. She had chosen them in preference to expensive blooms from a florist, thinking sentimentally that Harry would prefer the wild flowers of the Tyrol which he had known so well. She noticed that the nosegay was a little withered. Today she would gather fresh ones.

She picked up the silver frame and studied anew the dearly-loved features. Harry had been dark as she was herself, except that her skin was white and his had been olive. He had the black, melting eyes of a Latin and his white, even teeth were revealed in his smile. The photographer who had displayed the picture in his window had been approached by a dental paste manufacturer to buy the portrait for an advertisement. Naturally Harry had refused, but his modelling potentialities had been a joke between them.

Harry had been sultry and overwhelming, almost

domineering, but Evelyn had enjoyed being submissive. A man, she thought, should be masterful. That in marriage he might become too much so never occurred to her. Only in the matter of delaying their wedding had she ever opposed him. It had not seemed much to ask for a year when he was to have the rest of her life. That had gone down badly. Harry had been strongly sexed, and in the frank modern manner had been quite open about it. It was what made him so eager for consummation.

'You're putting an unnecessary strain upon us both,' he had grumbled. 'I'm a virile man and you aren't frigid, thank goodness, so why won't you . . .?'

But she had refused to anticipate marriage, feeling such an action would degrade her love and spoil the climax of her wedding day. She had been able to sublimate her passions in music. Never had she played so splendidly as during those last months, but Harry had no music to relieve his feelings, only, he told her whimsically, cold baths.

Then had come the suggestion of the roadhouse on that last night, which had offended her fastidiousness. Her refusal had sent Harry to his death. That had haunted her ever since. If she had not refused him the accident might not have occurred.

But although he had been so against allowing her to leave him to tour Europe, he often left her himself to fulfil his skiing commitments, and he never suggested that she should accompany him. Deep in her musical studies and disliking snow, she had had no wish to do so. He always returned glowing with health and victories, declaring how much he had missed her. She never gave a thought as to whom he met abroad, nor was she jealous of his friends, but he had been very jealous of her many admirers, and demanded repeated assurances of her fidelity. That she had promised him for always, and that meant even after his death.

Thus she had been deeply shocked to discover that although she had dedicated herself to Harry's memory, her senses could respond to a man's embrace. She had believed that part of her was dead for ever. Now, as she recalled Max's lovemaking, a sensuous warmth suffused her at the memory of the close pressure of his lips, and the grip of his arms. Her eyes on the portrait, she said contritely:

'Forgive me, Harry.'

Max had declared that her fiancé would not have expected her to live on in solitude and would want her to find new happiness if she could. If she had been the one to go, she could not kid herself that Harry would not have replaced her. As she had told Max, men were men, but she had felt no urge to replace Harry.

'A cult and yourself its high priestess.' Max's mocking voice seemed to ring in her ears. Had she really been acting a part, seeing herself like Tennyson's Mariana immured in her moated grange, wishing she were dead? If she were truly honest, she had to admit that the sharp edge of her grief had dulled long ago, and her apathy had become a habit. She would never forget Harry, but that part of her life was over, she had passed on to a new phase.

It was Max who was forcing her to face the truth, dragging her out of her self-absorption, making her feel.

From the dead man her thoughts went to the living one. What was motivating Max to cause him to go to such lengths to rouse her? She could find nothing in herself to appeal to him. The picture he had drawn of the girl he might one day marry was of someone soft and clinging, whom he felt an urge to protect. She herself was no vine,

77

and did not need protection, though she had delighted in Harry's masculine arrogance. She knew nothing about Max except that he was apparently in affluent circumstances and was in Seefeld on holiday. Somehow he had won Amy's approval, but perhaps he had been more expansive to her aunt than to herself. He had friends in Innsbruck, but he did not seem deeply involved with them, nor with anyone else. Perhaps he was at a loose end and she had intrigued him by her aloofness. Another girl might have fallen for him at sight; probably many did when he honoured them with his attentions.

That must be it. She presented a new diversion, while flattering his vanity as a worker of miracles. The resurrection of Evelyn Rivers was a challenge, and to that end he had exerted his charm and persuasiveness, even using the lure of sex. That he had been partially successful was annoying, but after what she had said to him yesterday, he would leave her alone. At least he did not know about Evelina Ravelli. She, poor creature, was dead as mutton and could never be revived.

Replacing the photograph, she looked down at her hand, lying upon the feather overlay which, in Austria, did duty for sheets and blankets. Though she strove to keep alive the memory of Harry, she had no memento of that other side of her life. Her piano at her request had been sold. The television set was banished to her father's study. She never heard music if she could possibly avoid it. Max must have noticed that her left hand was not normal, but he had never referred to it. No doubt he connected it with the accident, but he did not know its significance. That was one thing he had not been able to probe with his questions and his bullying. The fact that she had kept that secret from him gave her a perverse satisfaction.

Childish voices rose from beneath her window. Jane and Bobby were up early to greet the new day. She must make amends to them for her unresponsiveness yesterday, for she really did like children, in spite of what she had said to Max. Her loneliness had been largely her own fault, but it had needed Max's intervention to open her eyes to the fact. He had done her that much good, she allowed grudgingly, but she did not want to see him again and be exposed to any further taunts.

So she assured herself, without much conviction, as she went to run her bath.

It had rained in the night, and the morning was grey, with misty wreaths trailing over the mountains, alternately obscuring and revealing their peaks. Evelyn wandered about the lounge and terrace, until she realized that she was secretly hoping Max would appear after all, and that sent her scurrying down to the shops to make some unnecessary purchases. A useless precaution, for he had not turned up during her absence, thereby confirming her assumption that he had had more than enough of her.

The sun came out in the afternoon, and remembering that she wanted to find some more flowers, Evelyn asked Amy to accompany her on to the green park-like slopes opposite to the hotel. Here there were seats dotted about, and on the farther side, the slope descended more gradually to a wide valley, with houses clustered around an octagonal church.

Amy sat on a seat while Evelyn picked some of the yellow oxlip-like flowers which grew plentifully everywhere. When she had collected the few she needed, she joined her aunt on the seat. Amy eyed the blooms dourly. She had been into Evelyn's room and seen the enshrined photograph. But it was of Max whom she spoke.

'Such a charming man, and you know, dear, I think

he's very taken with you.'

'Then you know more than I do,' Evelyn returned tartly, 'and anyway, I've no use for him.'

Amy sighed. 'You should take more notice of the people about you. You're still only a young girl, darling, and it's time you should be thinking of marriage again.'

It was more than she had ever dared to say before, and she watched anxiously for her niece's reaction to her words.

'I shall never marry,' Evelyn said firmly. 'I should feel unfaithful to Harry if I did.'

'But he wasn't faithful to you.'

Evelyn turned slowly round to stare at her aunt.

'What did you say?' she asked blankly.

'I always said you ought to be told,' Amy went on steadily. 'But your parents were against it. I can't stand it any longer – watching you make a fetish of a most undeserving person.'

'I don't believe you,' Evelyn said flatly. 'And you should be ashamed to speak ill of the dead.'

'God knows, I don't want to run down poor Harry when he can't defend himself,' Amy declared fervently, 'but had you no suspicion? All those trips abroad to ski competitions. Do you imagine he was always alone?'

Evelyn was silent, remembering. Harry returned from those excursions with an apologetic air – she thought it was because he hated having to leave her. He always brought her an expensive present – wasn't that what the deceiver was supposed to do? There had been something a little furtive in his expression while he had described his doings. With his temperament, it was just possible . . .

'Who told you?' she demanded abruptly.

'It was common knowledge, though of course no one said anything to you.'

'Oh, just hearsay,' Evelyn said contemptuously.

'It was more than that, dear, and Max...'

'Max?' Evelyn interrupted. 'What's it got to do with him?'

'Max skis too,' Amy pointed out. 'Of course he'd heard of Harry – everyone interested in the sport had, he was so celebrated. I don't think Max ever actually met him, but he knew his name and his reputation.'

'And is that what you both discussed when I'd gone to bed?' Evelyn asked angrily. 'Pulling Harry to pieces between you? It was horrid of you!'

'We did no such thing,' Amy returned with spirit. 'He asked who Harry was – apparently you yourself had mentioned him.' ... During the dance, when she had been so bemused ... Evelyn drooped her head in shame. 'So I told him. He remembered the name and he said it was a pity you should be wasting your devotion upon the memory of such a womanizer.'

'Yes, Max is very hot on waste,' Evelyn said bitterly. How amused Max must have been by her assertions, her declaration that their love had been a wonderful thing, well knowing that Harry had been deceiving her. It must have added spice to his dealings with her. Perhaps he imagined that she was another of the same sort and had kissed her to find out. He must have thought she was incredibly naïve and innocent never to have guessed, but why should she? She was not naturally suspicious and her music had absorbed her during Harry's absences.

'I hope that in the course of your revelations you didn't disclose the fact that I'm a pianist who can no longer play,' she said icily.

'That was not necessary,' Amy said quietly. 'I made no revelations, Eve, beyond Harry's surname.'

Which was what Max himself had said.

'Well, that's something to be thankful for,' Evelyn conceded.

She stared disconsolately up the steep slope to their left, where the chair lift was toiling slowly to take visitors to view the scene from the top, and suddenly realized that it was a ski-run, that Harry might even have skimmed down it during one of those tours about which, she recollected now, he had always been somewhat reticent. Who had waited for him to make the descent, stayed with him perhaps at one of the hotels, maybe the very one where Max was lodging now? She knew that Amy would not have told her unless she had been very sure of her facts, and Max had confirmed them. The handsome English champion's love affairs must have been common knowledge in the Tyrol.

'I'm sorry, dear,' Amy said gently.

'You needn't be,' Evelyn told her. 'You're quite right, I ought to have been told when I went on making such an ass of myself. Dedicating myself to his memory!' She laughed drearily. 'Of course I loved him, nothing can alter that. Apparently plenty of other women did too. We all share a common memory of someone who was gay, gallant, and completely faithless.'

She let the flowers fall upon the grass. The discovery of Harry's perfidy had come too late to hurt her, but the knowledge that Max had known of it humiliated her deeply.

She stood up, shaking out her skirt.

'Do you mind if I go off on my own, Auntie? I ... I've rather a lot to think about.'

She walked along by the Wildsee and turned up the wooded path that led uphill to the right of it. She walked for a long way, and by the time she returned, she had finally thrown off the thraldom of the past. Re-entering her room, she took Harry's photograph from beside her bed and put it away in her suitcase.

Max had known that Harry had betrayed her love, but although he had been irritated by her attitude, he had not enlightened her. In fact he had told her that she was fortunate that her romance had ended without disillusion, for if Harry had lived, disillusionment would have been inevitable sooner or later. That was a point in Max's favour.

She began to wish that she had not snubbed him so severely. Amy had declared that he was taken with her, and men were not tempted to kiss girls they found unattractive. A little warm glow relieved the soreness of her heart. If only he would come again she would give him a very different reception.

Amy decided that next day they would go to Innsbruck. They left on the morning train, armed with the packed lunch with which the Haus Clara obligingly provided its guests when they went out for the day, for meals in restaurants were very expensive.

Past Reith, the line wound along the side of a mountain, with a wooded gorge on the right, on the opposite side of which the road which they had traversed on their way to the Brenner ran parallel with the railway. It went through tunnels and showed occasional glimpses of rocky clefts in the sides of the mountain, down some of which were waterfalls. At one point, the line crossed the gorge over a bridge and then began the descent into the Inn Valley. Startling glimpses of peaks appeared from time to time, and Amy remarked:

'I suppose if one lived here there would come a time when one didn't notice the mountains.'

'Isn't that true of most familiar things?' Evelyn suggested. 'But for all that the Tyrolese are very devoted to their mountains.'

She was thinking of Max, as she usually did now. Was he Tyrolese? He had mentioned Vienna, where he apparently lived, and the Viennese came into a different category. Gay, lighthearted people, she had always supposed, who were associated in her mind with Strauss waltzes and musical comedy hussars. But it must be very changed now after the devastation of the last war. It had been a Strauss waltz which she had been dancing to when she called Max Harry. A truly musical comedy situation, she thought wryly. Vaguely she wondered if Strauss was the extent of his musical appreciation – at least it was better than 'pop' which she abhorred.

'I don't suppose,' she murmured, 'that Max is musical.'

'Why? What made you think of that?' Amy asked, looking startled.

'Oh, I just wondered.'

Amy hesitated, but decided to hold her tongue.

The train passed through the outskirts of Innsbruck, and after a brief halt at the Westernbahnhof, pulled into the main station.

Amy knew the town and headed for the old part of it, which she said was the most interesting. They reached the Mariatheresiastrasse, which presents the most familiar view of Innsbruck, with the Saint Anne column in the foreground and the great wall of the Nordkette rising up behind it. They crossed the Marktgraben, and a narrow street led them into a sunny square, surrounded by stone arcades, presided over by the much advertised 'Golden Roof', which actually looked a little tarnished. It covered a balcony protruding from the second floor of an ancient house. All the houses surrounding the square were old, many with flower-filled window boxes and shutters to their windows. On a corner stood the Heibling House, with four tiers of bay windows above the arches of the arcade, a marvel in pale-pink rococo. After pausing to admire, Amy led the way down a narrow street into the Square of the Dom, which was small, paved and peaceful. She mounted the steps of the church of that name, with its twin towers each crowned with a copper 'onion', and gently pushed open the heavy wooden door, beckoning to Evelyn to look within.

Evelyn caught her breath as the glittering spectacle of the high altar drew her gaze. Glistening gold appeared to reach from floor to vaulted roof. Later when they explored the church, the wealth of ornament appeared a little tawdry, there was too much of it, but that first glimpse had been a vision of Eldorado. They visited other churches, including the Hofkirche, with the enormous tomb of the Emperor Maximilian filling the centre of the nave, guarded on either side by a line of massive bronze figures representing his supposed ancestors, including one of England's King Arthur in full armour.

Tired of sightseeing, Amy did a little shopping, and when she had finished, they turned into the wide space before the Imperial Palace which had once housed the Dukes of Tyrol. The long ochre-tinted façade, with its ornamental clipped trees between each ground floor window, went down one side. The theatre approached by steps was on the other, flanked by Leopold's fountain, on top of which he was depicted upon a prancing steed, with an attendant nymph on each corner of the water-filled basin below. The red seats surrounding it looked inviting, but Amy opted for the gardens beyond, which would be quieter and more secluded, and they could eat their lunch in peace.

It was a pretty park, with the Nordkette filling in the background. The cliff below the snowline looked so like a grey cloud that more than once Evelyn found herself thinking that rain was coming up. But the sky above the mountain was clear blue, and the sun shone on green lawns and massed flowers.

Their lunch eaten, Amy became immersed in a pattern book which she had bought, and Evelyn idly scanned the passers-by. Green sward separated them from a more distant walk, which emerged from a group of trees and disappeared behind a colour-filled flower bed. For a stretch of several dozen yards, promenaders along it were clearly visible in the bright light from where Evelyn was sitting in the shade of a spreading beech.

Suddenly she grew tense, her eyes riveted upon a couple who had appeared upon that path. The man she recognized at once; he was unmistakable, although he was wearing a grey suit in which she had not seen him before. A girl was clinging to his arm, a small girl, the top of her bright golden head barely reached his shoulder. She wore a frilly blue dress, somewhat over-flounced for modern fashions, and blue sandals. She was too far away for Evelyn to distinguish her features, but she appeared to be young and pretty.

Although Evelyn had been given to understand there was a girl in Max's life, she had been somewhat nebulous. Seeing her in the flesh, when she had begun to think more kindly, even sentimentally, about him, was like a douche of cold water.

It also raised conjectures. She must belong to the friends in Innsbruck whom Max had mentioned, and it was her sandals which had been left in his car, perhaps the very pair that she was wearing now, for Evelyn had returned them when she had said good-bye. Max could not really have forgotten to whom they belonged. She saw in her mind's eye the stretch of crocus-strewn meadow and the blue-clad girl skipping gaily across it, perhaps being lifted over the stream, which had had such ill consequences for herself. The girl loked so small and delicate, Max could carry her for miles with ease. No doubt her fragility evoked all that protective chivalry about which Max had talked so much. The surprising thing was that she was keeping him dangling. Max was a prize most girls would be eager to snap up. Their attitudes as they went past, the proprietorial way in which she clung to his arm indicated that she regarded him as her property. Why did she not make sure of him, instead of leaving him free to wander after other girls? Possibly she was a vain little coquette and enjoyed playing with his feelings. She looked as if she might be, Evelyn decided scornfully, unwilling to admit that what was pricking her was jealousy.

She glanced at her aunt, but Amy apparently had noticed nothing; she was intent upon perusing her book. The couple had passed out of sight when she looked up to say:

'I like the design of that sweater. I think I'll try it. It would be nice for you, dear, and I suppose you would like it to be in black or white?'

'No,' Evelyn exclaimed vehemently. 'Make it scarlet!'

Amy stared at her in speechless astonishment, then she beamed. 'Do you really mean that?'

'Yes, I do,' Evelyn assured her. 'I'm sick of being a drab.'

She had used to look so well in colours. She remembered a flame-coloured dress which she had once worn, which Harry had admired, saying it contrasted so well with her black hair and eyes, her matt-white skin. Not that he often noticed her clothes, but that night he had been sufficiently impressed to quote poetry.

> 'Red oranges that glow with life,
> Like youth's passion, storm and strife.'

'You positively glow, darling.'

She had glowed with life, and she had experienced youth's passion, storm and strife. But the glow had faded to ashes, until Max had blown upon them and the fires had started to revive. That petite blonde had suffered no eclipse, she was fresh and unspoiled, and Max appeared to find her charming.

Amy's gentle voice broke into her whirling thoughts.

'Were you serious about having a red jumper? I don't want to buy the wool and find you've changed your mind.'

'I shan't do that,' Evelyn said positively. 'It's time I wore colours again.'

'High time,' Amy agreed. She looked at her niece narrowly. 'I shouldn't worry about that little girl,' she went on comfortably. 'She could never hold a man like Max. A little flirtation, I should imagine, though his attitude looked almost paternal to me.'

So Amy *had* seen Max and his girl-friend pass.

'I'm not in the least worried,' Evelyn told her haughtily. 'I haven't the slightest interest in Max Linden's affairs.'

'Eve, Eve, do you think I'm blind?' Amy chuckled. 'And I haven't lived for over fifty years without developing some perspicacity. Max holds ... I mean I think he holds ... a quite important position. He needs a wife capable of entertaining his associates. You would fit the bill admirably. Do you suppose it hasn't occurred to him?'

'But I wouldn't want to marry because I'd make a good hostess,' Evelyn objected, 'and I don't suppose I would, not now.'

'Max is quite shrewd enough to recognize your potentialities,' Amy insisted, 'and men of his age have passed the period of wild infatuations, at least when it comes to choosing a wife.'

'What nonsense we're talking!' Evelyn exclaimed, her colour rising. Marriage and Max? Amy was allowing her romantic notions to run away with her. 'After ... after what you told me yesterday, I'm off men,' she concluded.

'That's why I told you,' Amy said calmly. 'I saw something was developing between you and Max and I didn't see why Harry's memory should stand between you. He did you far too much harm for much too long, without spoiling your chance of finding real happiness.'

'I think you're rushing to all sorts of conclusions without any grounds,' Evelyn cried emphatically. 'What makes you think I'd be happy with Max? He ... he hasn't been very nice to me.'

'You probably misunderstood him,' Amy told her. 'It's a common failing with people in love.'

'But I'm not ...' Evelyn gasped, and broke off. Could it possibly be true? Was she falling in love with Max and that was why the sight of the blonde had disturbed her so? He had certainly obsessed her thinking ever since she had met him, but that physical thing in the crocus field was not love, though it could have been a beginning. But it was not how Max had defined love. She remembered how she had thought his talk of consideration and cherishing left something out, and suddenly she understood.

He felt tender towards his little doll, but his virile nature required something more exciting to satisfy its needs. So like Harry, he took his fun on the side while he waited for his intended to make up her mind. After all, Harry had always returned to her. Did Max always go back to his blonde when he had strayed? But she did not want to become involved with another of that breed, and Amy's suggestion that when it came to marriage Max would select a suitable figurehead was not inspiring. It was typical of a man about town with his wife installed in his home to entertain his guests, and his lady friends elsewhere.

Amy said insinuatingly: 'You used to look so lovely, Eve. That little girl couldn't hold a candle to you if you wanted to cut her out.'

'She's got what I haven't got any longer,' Evelyn said bitterly, 'freshness, and a heart no other man has touched.'

'Oh, stuff,' Amy ejaculated. 'Freshness in blondes soon wears off, and I don't think Max would appreciate naïveté.'

Possibly true, Evelyn thought, and she had once been the object of much male admiration, but wanting only Harry she had repulsed all overtures, though it pleased her to know that she was desirable; it made her gift of herself to Harry seem more valuable.

Could any man still find her desirable, she mused, when she had lost her biggest asset, the glamour of the concert platform? Possibly if she chose to exert herself, she could detach Max from his little doll, since he seemed to be susceptible ... She checked her thoughts sharply. Run after Max when he had treated her so casually, finding diversion in stirring her emotions, dissecting her as if she had been a laboratory specimen? Amy did not know how completely callous he was, or she would not talk of finding happiness with him, nor could she, if she were in her right mind, allow herself to love him.

Then she remembered something which she had overlooked.

'All this is beside the point,' she said coolly, 'because Max has finished with us. We ... er ... quarrelled during our Brenner trip. I told him once we were home I wouldn't speak to him again.'

'I don't suppose he'll take any notice of that,' Amy remarked cheerfully. 'What did you quarrel about?'

'We don't see eye to eye about a lot of things,' Evelyn told her evasively.

Amy glanced at her shrewdly, but made no comment. If her niece had reached the point of quarrelling with Max it suggested they had attained some degree of intimacy. A confirmed match-maker, she was convinced that a husband was the answer to Evelyn's problems, and not only had Max shown a great interest in her, but he was more than eligible. A firm believer in her own intuition, she was convinced that he could not be anything but honest, even if he did promenade in the park with flirtatious blondes.

Anxious to escape further questioning, Evelyn suggested it was time they went for their train, and Amy replaced her book in her bag.

'And of course the red jumper has nothing to do with Max?' she asked slyly.

'Certainly not,' Evelyn told her with too much emphasis. 'You don't suppose that it's on his account that I've decided to wear colours again?'

Amy said nothing. She knew very well it was.

The day ended with the presentation of the small gifts

which Evelyn had bought for the children to make amends for her former snubbing. These were in the form of a little Tyrolean doll for Jane and a knife in a leather sheath for Bobby. About this last, she had had some misgivings, but Amy, who seemed to have inside information, assured her that it was what the boy was yearning for. He was delighted with it and said he was going to carve animals like the ones in the shops, and went off to find a piece of wood.

Mrs. Lambert, who was present at the gift offering, remarked cheerfully that she hoped he would not carve up Jane, but did not seem in the least disturbed by the prospect. She thanked Evelyn profusely, and said vaguely that she must not let the children become a nuisance.

Next morning, since Amy seemed convinced that Max would put in an appearance, Evelyn accepted Jake's invitation to go swimming, with more enthusiasm than she actually felt. If Max did turn up, she did not want him to think that she spent her time watching for him.

Upon hearing of her intention, Amy protested vigorously. She did not want Max to arrive and find her niece had gone out with another man, which was precisely what Evelyn hoped he would do. The water, Amy said, was too cold for outdoor swimming, Evelyn might take a chill, and she had not swum for a long time.

'Quite time I took it up again,' Evelyn returned, 'and the water in the pool is heated.'

She departed with Jake, wearing a skimpy shift over her swimsuit, waving her towel to her aunt, who was left sitting disconsolately upon the terrace.

CHAPTER FIVE

IT was very pleasant in the swimming pool and Evelyn, who had been a good swimmer, found her skill had not deserted her. Jake, himself an indifferent performer, was loud in admiration of her performance.

Afterwards she sat beside him upon her towel spread over the boards provided for sunbathing, and rubbed lotion vigorously into her skin.

'Now perhaps I'll look less like a corpse,' she told him.

She did not like bikinis, deeming them unworkmanlike, and her costume was plain regulation black. It emphasized the whiteness of her limbs. Her hair, released from her bathing cap, streamed over her shoulders, reaching to past her waist.

'What extraordinary things you do say!' Jake exclaimed. 'You've got a lovely skin. It's like magnolia petals.' He smiled shyly. 'We've got a magnolia in our garden. My dad's awfully proud of it.'

'Do you often compare your girl-friends to it?' she asked, laughing. 'They must be flattered.'

'Oh, no, I've never thought of it before. You don't think I'm being silly? It really is, you know, and you're the first girl I've met with a magnolia skin. But you must be careful,' he assumed a practical air to cover his poetic lapse. 'You mustn't let it burn too quickly.'

'I shan't do that. I don't want to look like a lobster. Rather a descent, from magnolias to shellfish!' She lay down, pushing her hair back from her shoulders. 'I haven't sunbathed since . . . Oh, for ages.'

Not since the summer before the accident, when she had acquired a lovely tan. Harry had called her 'Carmen.'

Jake's eyes were upon her left hand; for once she was not wearing a glove. He noticed the missing fingertip.

'I say, what did that? Was it an accident?'

For a moment murder looked out of her eyes. No one during the past two years had dared to comment upon her injury, except for the medical consultations. Then she recovered herself.

'Yes, it was an accident.'

'Does it inconvenience you at all?'

She passed her hand before her face the better to see it, and smiled wryly.

'Hardly at all.'

Something in her voice made him look at her anxiously.

'You didn't mind me mentioning it? It seems such hard luck.'

'I might have lost my arm,' she told him, 'that would have been much worse.'

But the net result was the same – no more bass chords, no more flying arpeggios.

'Yes, I suppose so.' Jake agreed, 'but it seems a pity.' What he meant was that he was distressed to see even so small a flaw upon a perfect thing.

'Yes,' Eve agreed. 'It was a pity.' She sprang to her feet. 'I must be getting back.'

He looked up at her long-limbed graceful figure from the board upon which he was gently roasting.

'Must you? It's so nice here.'

'I've left my aunt all alone.'

His eyes widened in wonder. 'Surely the old girl can look after herself? You don't have to bother about her?'

'I don't have to do anything, but she's been very kind to me.'

'I think you're a very nice person,' Jake said, sitting up.

Another couple came towards them, carrying a transistor which was blaring out a popular song. Evelyn shuddered.

'That's spoilt it,' she declared. 'I'm certainly going.'

Jake got up to join her. 'Don't you like it?' he asked. 'But perhaps you're not musical?'

'No,' Evelyn agreed, smiling, 'I can't be, can I?'

They left the seclusion of the fenced-round bathing pool and walked along the road back towards the town. Jake wore only his shorts, with a towel draped over his shoulders. Evelyn had put on sandals and re-donned her skimpy white dress which she found cooler than trousers. They mingled with the tourist visitors sauntering by in various stages of undress and peeling sunburn. It was a really hot day, and the mountains were sharp grey ramparts against an azure sky; the grass on the nearby slopes was a brilliant green.

A big car came gliding along the road, and braked to a sudden halt a few yards ahead of them. Evelyn recognized it with a lurch of her heart. Max jumped out of the driver's seat and stood on the path to waylay them. He was wearing the grey suit which he had had on in the gardens at Innsbruck, thereby confirming that she could not have possibly mistaken his identity. She tried to whip up some indignation at his effrontery in daring to accost her, when she had told him she did not want to speak to him again, but was guiltily glad that he had not taken her at her word, as Amy had insisted that he would not.

He was not, however, looking at her, but at Jake.

'*Grüss Gott,* Eve, you are out early this morning,' he

said crisply. 'We are on our way to call upon you.'

Evelyn hastened to explain her untidy appearance by saying she had been swimming. She was acutely aware of the girl sitting in the front seat of the car, a girl who when Max opened the door smiled at them vaguely.

'Is that your friend, Max?' she asked, but she did not look towards Evelyn. 'Please to introduce me.'

She put out a hand with an uncertain gesture, and Max put it into Evelyn's. It was very small and trembled in her clasp like a frightened bird. A hand which could not stretch an octave. Evelyn quickly released it and looked curiously at its owner. She was, of course, the girl she had seen with Max in the park. Close to she did not look so young; there was a quaint air of maturity about her. though her pretty face was still childishly round. She was beautifully turned out, again in blue, with matching sandals, a blue crinoline straw hat which shaded her eyes, and even blue lacy gloves. She knows it suits her to be feminine, Evelyn thought; she would look nothing in sports clothes. Doubtless too she knew that Max liked her full skirts and fragile fripperies. Did any man really appreciate a woman in trousers? She became acutely conscious of her own unruly appearance; bare-armed, bare-legged, her hair cascading down her back: she saw Max was looking at it with interest.

The girl's name was Sophia Hartmann, and Max addressed her as Sophy. Jake, whom lack of confidence was making brash, announced his own name loudly, and again Sophy's fluttering hand was caught and presented to him. The girl was a near-imbecile, Evelyn decided, or else she was really very clever. Those little fluttering movements were rather attractive ... to a man. Sophy looked so delicate and frail that she made Evelyn feel big and clumsy beside her.

She said in her soft voice – her English was only slightly accented – 'I have so much wanted to meet you, Fräulein Rivers. Max has told me so much about you.'

Evelyn wondered what. Definitely not everything, she thought dryly, and looked at Max to see if he showed any embarrassment, but he was studying Jake with undisguised antipathy.

'We thought we might ask you to take coffee with us.' Sophy went on, 'and also the good lady your aunt, whom Max says is most amiable.' Her English was a little stilted. 'But first we must go to find her.'

Evelyn thanked her and said Amy was at the hotel, and she must make herself respectable before she could go anywhere, repeating for Sophy's benefit that she had been swimming.

'That must be delightful,' Sophy exclaimed. 'I have often wished that I could swim.' Her small face was wistful.

'You could learn . . .' Evelyn began.

Sophy shook her head. '*Ach*, no. The sports are not for me.'

Evelyn thought that Max had certainly landed himself with a clinging vine. Her spirits rose; he could not be seriously enamoured of this quaint little doll. He might like to feel protective towards his women, but he also needed fire and passion. There was no fire in Sophy, apparently, though one could not be sure. Little women sometimes erupted like volcanoes.

Jake, who was feeling rather out of his depth with these expensive-looking people, excused himself, saying he must see what his sister was doing.

'See you later,' he said to Evelyn, and sauntered off. Max scowled at his retreating figure.

'What is it, Max?' Sophy asked. She seemed able to

sense his moods. 'Has something annoyed you?'

'Nothing, *liebling*,' he returned gently, then said curtly to Evelyn, as he opened the rear door, 'Will you please to get in?'

'No, thank you, I can cut across the field and I'll be at the hotel as soon as you will,' she returned, annoyed by his tone. He changed his note when the girl-friend was around, she thought wryly. 'I'm not fit to get into anybody's car like this.'

She ran off before he could remonstrate.

She did arrive before the big car had made the detour necessary to bring it up in front of Haus Clara. Amy was sitting on the terrace and was delighted by Max's invitation, as Evelyn had known she would be, thereby making any evasion upon her own part practically impossible. Though she was secretly pleased to see Max again, she did not think she was going to enjoy the society of his girl-friend.

Going upstairs to change, she rummaged disconsolately through her collection of drab-coloured garments looking for something attractive to put on. She possessed nothing which would compare with Sophy's dainty garments, and her white trousers were still at the cleaners. Suddenly realizing what was motivating her, she stared at her reflection in the mirror. The tall, dark girl who confronted her could not possibly rival Sophy's porcelain prettiness, nor did she want to, she thought angrily. Perversely she selected a pair of grey linen slacks and a black shirt which did nothing for her at all. She was sure Max would hate that black shirt.

Sure enough he raised his brows when she appeared with an expression as forbidding as her clothes, while Amy said despairingly:

'Eve dear, couldn't you have found something less

dreary to put on?'

'I thought this was very suitable casual wear,' Evelyn remarked offhandedly.

Max said: 'I would like so much to see you in colours.'

'I'm afraid I selected my wardrobe before I met you,' Evelyn returned, 'and I didn't . . . don't wear colours.'

She met Max's quizzical look with a defiant toss of her head.

Amy muttered: 'What about that scarlet jumper?' but Evelyn pretended not to have heard and turned to get into the car. She hoped Max had not heard her aunt's question, but from the sudden amused glint in his eyes, she was afraid that he had.

He drove through the town taking the Leutasch Road and up among the new buildings being erected among the wooded slopes overlooking the Seefeld plateau. The place he took them to had huge plate-glass windows in the lounge framing a view of the Seefelder, Reitherspitze and Harmelekopt peaks opposite. He seemed to be well known there and the proprietor greeted him enthusiastically. He brought Sophy in on his arm, which she had taken when he helped her out of the car. Evelyn thought she was rather overdoing the clinging act.

Max guided Sophy into a chair, then pulled one out for Amy. Evelyn found one for herself. She took a perverse pleasure in being neglected. On the Dolomite expedition she had had all Max's attention; today he was solicitous only for the other girl, thereby proving that Amy's deductions had been all wrong. She glanced at her aunt, and saw she was watching Sophy with a thoughtful expression. Was she realizing how mistaken she had been?

Coffee and a trolley bearing delicious cakes was

brought to them. Sophy smiled at Max.

'Choose one for me, dear.'

He made his selection, putting it upon her plate, and poured out her coffee for her, for it was served in individual pots. Evelyn regarded his attentions slightly scornfully. Could the girl do nothing for herself?

Sophy began to ask about their excursion to the Dolomites, betraying that Max had made no secret of it. Forgetting her pique, Evelyn described her impressions with enthusiasm. The Austrian girl listened with the same wistful expression which she had worn when she talked about swimming, and when Evelyn ceased, she remarked:

'You describe it so vividly, I can imagine it all.'

'But haven't you . . .' Evelyn began, unable to believe that Max had not taken Sophy up to the crocus field. She broke off, aware of a sudden tension in the air, and glancing at Max, saw he was watching Sophy with deep compassion in his eyes. Amy cleared her throat, and Sophy said composedly:

'No, *Fräulein*, it is useless for me to go, because I cannot see.'

'Oh!' It was no more than an almost soundless expulsion of breath, while Evelyn wondered how she could have been so dim. Her criticisms and resentments were drowned in a flood of compassion, but as if fearing she might seek to express it, Max gave her a warning glance. Sophy did not want pity.

He put his hand over the girl's and said gently:

'But you soon will, *liebchen*,' and explained to the other two, 'Sophy has been examined by a great ophthalmic surgeon. He thinks that he can perform . . . a miracle.'

Sophy shivered. 'Not a miracle, Max,' she corrected

him. 'Merely a long and intricate operation, but I am a great coward.' She smiled pathetically. 'I dread to have it done.'

'You are no coward, Sophy, you are the bravest girl I know,' Max assured her. 'And remember what it will mean to you.'

'I think it means even more to you,' Sophy said softly. 'You know that it is for your sake that I have consented.' She drew her hand away from under his, and turned towards where she sensed the other two were sitting.

'Max is very bad to speak of it when we are all enjoying ourselves,' she complained. 'But he wants you to know so you do not have too much sorrow for me, and I am a very lucky girl in many ways.' Her smile was beatific. 'Shall we not talk of other things?'

Amy promptly obliged with a flood of small talk, at which she was adept, and Sophy followed her lead with laughter and chatter. Her gaiety was remarkable and she managed her fork and cup with deft practised movements. No one glancing at her casually would suspect her handicap.

Evelyn watched her with admiration, her own thoughts chaotic. So much had been explained by Sophy's revelation. No wonder Max wanted to protect and serve her; she appealed to all that was best and most chivalrous in him. It was also clear why Sophy had hesitated to accept him. She wanted to be sure that the operation would be a success before she agreed to marry him.

Far from being a vapid doll, Sophy had pluck and grit. She obviously adored Max, but she would not let herself be a burden to him and had consented to face an ordeal which she dreaded solely so that she could become his wife.

For it transpired that Sophy never had had clear vision

and what she had never had she did not really miss, though it precluded her from doing so many things. She seemed happy within her limitations and managed to make the best of herself, but whatever transpired, Evelyn was sure her hold over Max was unbreakable, and he would never give her up.

Faced with Sophy's stoicism, she could well understand why Max had been so critical of herself. She flexed her left hand under the table, and smiled inwardly at her own folly, for she had bolstered her ego by reflecting that Max only knew the half of her story. Though he had shown her that her pose of inconsolable grief had become a sham, he was unaware that she had been deprived of a brilliant future. Lately she had begun to weave a day-dream in which she told him whom she had been and won his praise for her fortitude, for though he might deride her fidelity to a faithless man, he would understand the loss of a career.

She would never tell him now, for the loss of her piano-playing was trivial compared with Sophy's incapacity.

But Sophy had Max. He hung over her with tender devotion, ready to anticipate her needs. Watching them, Evelyn became aware that she would give anything, even her own sight, to be in Sophy's place. She had not been impressed by his definition of love until now, when she was seeing it in action. It would be so very heart-warming to draw comfort from his strength, and seek consolation in his arms, to be caressed, not demandingly, but with tenderness.

Bitterness burned up in her. How much she had missed while she had been indulging in her fantasy of deathless love, which was a myth, because Harry had cheated her, and in a lesser degree Max was cheating her too, for though he had made her live again, he had not offered the love which made life worth living.

He had done her no kindness by stripping away the veils of illusion which she had drawn between herself and the harshess of reality. By seeking to re-animate her atrophied emotions, he had awoken her to awareness of himself. Though perhaps not yet actually in love with him, she was on the verge of being so, and he had brought Sophy to meet her to show her he was committed elsewhere. Thus before it could flower, her new love was blighted.

She felt like the species of crab which lives in a borrowed shell and when it has outgrown its hospitable shelter must seek another abode, being in the meantime nakedly vulnerable. Bereft of Harry, shorn of her former glories, she had turned towards Max and been confronted with Sophy.

Max had been neither kind nor considerate towards her, but if he were accused of trifling with her affections, he would no doubt retort that she had benefited from his intervention.

'You're very quiet, Eve,' Amy said to her. 'Did our day in Innsbruck yesterday tire you?'

'Oh, were you in Innsbruck?' Sophy asked. 'I wish I had known of that. Max, why did you not bring them to see us?'

'Because I was spending the day with you,' Max reminded her.

'It was a lovely day,' Sophy said reminiscently, her vague blue eyes growing soft. 'But they must come another time. Where are you, Eva?' She used the German form of Evelyn's name, and held out her hand. Not knowing quite what was expected of her, Evelyn touched her fingers. 'Max says you are beautiful. I wish I could see you.'

'Max flatters me,' Evelyn told her, 'actually he referred to my bone structure. I may have been passable once, but now I'm definitely skeletal.' She threw Max a barbed glance.

He glooked pointedly at her black shirt.

'You do not try to enhance yourself,' he said dryly.

His eyes were hard; he was definitely displeased with her. No doubt he thought her garb was an indication that she was retreating back into her old obsessions. But she could not do that, even if she had wished to do so. She had emerged from her seclusion and there was no going back.

Sophy continued to insist that Evelyn and her aunt must come to tea with her family.

'I want all Max's friends to be my friends,' she said with a charming smile.

About to point out that they were not Max's friends, Evelyn checked herself, not knowing how else to explain her relationship with him, which was no relationship at all. Amy gave her a warning look, and declared that they would be delighted to come if Sophy would like to fix a day and an hour. Sophy expressed her pleasure, and insisted that Max should bring them.

'It will have to be soon,' she explained, 'because Max will be going back to Vienna.'

This news startled Evelyn. Her stay in Seefeld was indefinite, but she had not realized that Max's was not. The knowledge that he would soon be leaving brought to her an acute sense of loss. But he was no loss, she assured herself; his presence could only cause her discomfort and the sooner he went away the better it would be for all concerned.

She could think of no excuses to make for not going to visit the Hartmanns, while Amy and Sophy made the final arrangements, though she did not want to go. She was trying to adjust to the fact that after a few days she would never see Max again.

Max dropped them at the Haus Clara, and after taking leave of Sophy, and with a brief word of thanks to Max, Evelyn followed her aunt into the hotel. To her astonishment, she found Max was behind her as she stepped over the threshold.

He addressed himself to Amy.

'Sophy has something she wants to say to you, Mrs Banks.'

Amy looked surprised, but good-naturedly went back down the steps to the car. Evelyn made a movement towards the stairs – she had no wish to be alone with Max – but before she could gain them, he pushed her unceremoniously into the empty lounge.

'And I have something I want to say to you.' His expression was a little grim.

She raised her brows. 'Indeed?'

He looked disparagingly at her black shirt.

'Why will you wear such horrible clothes?' he asked.

'Really, Max, if that's all . . .' she began.

'*Ach*, no, it is not. It would be better if you sat down.'

'That sounds ominous,' she said lightly, sinking into an armchair and crossing one long leg over the other. He began to prowl up and down the space before the bar.

'That young man you were with this morning, how long have you known him?' he jerked over his shoulder at her.

'My dear Max, what on earth's that got to do with you?'

'Do not prevaricate,' he snapped.

It crossed her mind that he was annoyed because he was jealous of Jake. The thought elated her until she realized its absurdity. Why should Max be jealous when he had his adoring Sophy waiting for him outside?

'Not very long,' she admitted. 'Jake Armstrong is an estimable young man who happens to be holidaying in Seefeld. He asked me to go swimming with him. Any objection?'

'And that is all?'

'That's all. Except ... Oh, yes ... he told me my skin was like the magnolia his father grows in his suburban garden.'

'*Ach*, but that was impertinence!'

'Not at all, I thought it was rather nice, especially as I don't imagine he often manages such flights of fancy. Must be the effect of the romantic scenery.'

Max relaxed into a slow grin. 'I hope it will not produce more ambitious fancies,' he remarked. 'But I did not think you were the kind of girl who encouraged pick-ups.'

The colloquial expression sounded odd from him, whose English was usually so correct. Evelyn smiled mischievously.

'If I remember aright, I picked you up,' she said demurely, 'or you picked me up, whichever way you like to put it.'

'That was in unusual circumstances,' he countered, looking at her keenly. 'You needed me, *nicht wahr*?'

'Did I?' If Max had not been coming down the mountainside would she still be locked away in her moated grange, or would she in time have managed to release herself without his aid? Would Amy have brought herself to enlighten her about Harry without the impetus of Max's presence?

'I flatter myself you did,' Max countered. 'Where did you pick up this young swimmer?'

'He isn't a pick-up, he's staying here with us. Isn't that what you wanted? That I should return to normal life? Normal life means normal relations with young people. I haven't swum for two years. I enjoyed it.'

A look of keen satisfaction crossed Max's face, which killed any lingering hope that he might be jealous.

'There are perhaps other things which you used to enjoy that you would like to do again,' he suggested.

'Perhaps, I haven't really thought about it. My ... er ... resurrection has been rather sudden, you know.'

He turned away, thrusting his hands into his trouser pockets, and stared out of the window. With his back to her, he said with careful casualness:

'Your aunt mentioned that you were musical ...' she started, gripping her hands together. When had Amy told him that? ... 'I am going to a concert in Munich tomorrow night, at which Hans Schreiberg will be performing. He is making a reputation for himself as a pianist, and I want to hear him. His programme includes, I understand, some pieces by Liszt. I wondered if you would care to come along.'

If he had wanted to shock her back to normality, this was a means even more drastic than embracing her, but this time he had overdone it.

She stared at the back of his head with blank eyes, while her body seemed turned to stone. A concert ... pianist ... Liszt, they had all been forbidden words in her hearing. It was Liszt which she had played at her last concert, three of the Hungarian Rhapsodies, and the Totentanz. Before her mental vision rose the black and white keyboard of the concert grand, the spotlight wavering before her eyes; in her ears rose the thunders of applause, which changed to a sound like rushing water, and deadly nausea swept over her.

'Eve!'

She heard his voice from a long way off, the clink of a glass, she felt his hand at the back of her head, the rim of a tumbler against her lips.

'Drink this.'

She gulped the spirit which he was offering her, and gradually the mist cleared from before her vision, the tumultuous sounds died away, and with them her nausea.

'Better now?'

She became aware that he was kneeling before her, chafing her hands, and he looked intensely distressed.

'Oh, yes,' she laughed a little shakily. 'I . . . I must have turned faint, but at least I chose the right place to faint in.'

He stood up, picked up the glass and moved to replace it upon the bar counter.

'I have blundered again,' he muttered, adding more loudly: 'Forgive me.'

'It's for you to forgive me for being so stupid. I can't think what made me go like that,' she said glibly. She looked at him doubtfully, as he stood by the bar, half turned away from her. 'Did you . . . did you offer to take me to a concert?'

'Forget it.'

'Oh, please, I want to go.'

He swung round and she saw relief flash into his face.

'Oh, Max,' she cried, 'I'm just starved for music. I've been deprived of it far too long!'

It had been her first and purest love, but because she could no longer interpret it, she had childishly rejected it: since she could not create, she had denied it altogether, but now she knew how foolish she had been. Music could have comforted her, if only she had let it.

Max was looking at her oddly.

'Why were you deprived?'

Fearing she had betrayed too much, she said hurriedly:

'Circumstances were against it. But isn't Munich a long way to go?'

'Only about two hours by car, two and a half allowing for a hold-up at the frontier.'

He was still watching her curiously, and she knew her explanation had hardly been convincing, but it was all that she intended to offer him. She said conventionally:

'I would like to go very much, but wouldn't you rather take Miss Hartmann?'

'No, I would not,' he said so abruptly, that she was startled. He smiled. 'I should explain, she does not appreciate serious music, she would be very bored.'

'But you enjoy good music?' she asked wonderingly.

'I do, and I should like to share this experience with someone who also appreciates it.'

A flattering statement, yet she could not rid herself of an impression that he had some hidden motive for his invitation, which she could not divine. She looked at him dubiously. Was it by chance that he had asked her to hear a pianist play Liszt? But he could not possibly know that both the instrument and the composer had a special significance for her.

'I particularly want to hear this young man,' he explained, 'to discover if he is as good as he is said to be.'

She sighed, thinking quite without vanity that he would have to be very good to be better than Evelina Ravelli, but Max would never hear her.

'It is a long way to go on one's own,' he went on. 'So I hoped that you would honour me with your company.'

Nicely put and reasonable, since Sophy did not share

his taste. She experienced a little glow of pleasure to know that they had something in common. Amy must have given him a hint about her own preferences. She frowned a little as she recalled her aunt. Amy had been too eager to push her on to Max. Now that she knew he was committed, she would change her attitude. She might even deplore this jaunt to Munich.

Amy did. While Evelyn had been with Max, she had had a long intimate talk with Sophy, who seemed to have won her heart. She was, she said, so courageous and cheerful despite her disability. This Evelyn felt as a further prick, a reflection upon her own past conduct. Resentfully she mentioned Max's invitation to go to Munich.

Amy was dumbfounded. To go to a concert and run the risk of reopening old wounds seemed to her to be a dangerous experiment. The effect upon Evelyn might be shattering, but what was quite incomprehensible to her was Max's proposal to spend a long evening with another girl when he should be devoting himself to Sophy, since he would soon be far away from Innsbruck.

'I was quite wrong about her,' she admitted, 'but of course I had no idea. I'm afraid I misled you, darling, but since you assured me you haven't become involved with him there's no great harm done.'

She looked at her niece a little anxiously, fearing that she had raised hopes which could not be fulfilled.

'None whatever,' Evelyn assured her, 'but I don't see why I shouldn't go to Munich. Sophy isn't musical, apparently, and Max is.' She looked interrogatively at her aunt.

Amy moved uneasily. She knew very well that music was as important to Max as it had been to her niece. It was not only a diversion, but his livelihood. Apparently he had not disclosed that.

But for Evelina Ravelli to appear in public with a well-known musical director and concert promoter would be inviting comment. True, Evelina was probably forgotten by now, but someone might recognize her, and then what would Evelyn's reaction be?

'After all, they're not engaged,' Evelyn pointed out, mistaking the cause of Amy's worried look.

'But they soon will be,' Amy told her eagerly, for the Sophy-Max romance seemed to her to be utterly charming. 'And she'll be able to see – modern surgery does perform miracles, as Max said. Sophy's parents have known there was hope for her for some time, but she hesitated to undergo the operation. She fears the world may not be as beautiful as she imagines it to be.' Amy laughed. 'She really is sweet. Max finally persuaded her that she must have it done.'

'She seems to have confided a great deal to you in a short space of time,' Evelyn remarked. 'After all, you're a stranger.'

Amy smiled complacently. 'I flatter myself I have a sympathetic manner, and you were a long time.' She looked at Evelyn a little severely. 'You wouldn't like to come between Sophy and Max?'

'I'm sure I couldn't if I tried, but one evening out won't do that.'

'He didn't suggest I might come along as a chaperon?' Amy said meaningly.

'Chaperons are dead as dodos,' Evelyn said scornfully, 'and you know you'd be bored stiff.'

'I would,' Amy agreed, 'but Sophy is so sweet and brave, I should hate her to be hurt,' she added significantly.

Evelyn moved impatiently. Granted Sophy was brave and sweet, but Amy need not keep harping upon it.

'I'm not hurting her,' she said. 'He's probably told her all about it, as he did about the Brenner . . .' she stopped. looking conscious. Max would not have told Sophy all about the Brenner trip, and that episode was all the more reprehensible now she knew about the girl. But she need fear no repetition, now that Max had introduced her to Sophy. He had erected a barrier between them, which he must respect. She sighed a little. Max was no less attractive because he belonged to someone else. All the same she was determined to go to Munich. That posed the question – did her reactions mean that she was in love with him? Could one fall in love upon such short acquaintance? It had been known to happen. In which case, she would be wiser not to go, but since he would be returning to Vienna shortly, and their association would soon cease, she could not resist the urge to spend this one evening with him. Sophy could spare her that.

Meanwhile there was something which she must do before tomorrow night, and she hoped the dress shops in Seefeld would prove adequate for her needs.

CHAPTER SIX

EVELYN bought a dress in apricot brocade with touches of
green about the waist and low neckline. It fell in soft folds
to her feet and was cut upon the straight simple lines
which suited her tall, graceful figure. To go with it she
had purchased a green wool stole, gilt slippers, evening
bag and green gloves. Luckily she had spent little while
she had been abroad, and had ample travellers' cheques
to cover her needs.

The radiant image which her mirror reflected was a
complete contrast to the sombreness of her usual attire.
The colours enhanced the darkness of her eyes, and the
faint tan which she was beginning to acquire toned with
the golden shade of the dress.

Her hair gave her some trouble. It was straight and
very fine. The braid which she usually wore hanging over
one shoulder was too unsophisticated for evening wear. It
was a style which she had affected because it was no
trouble, but she was expending a great deal of care upon
her appearance tonight. Finally she coiled it into a knot
in the nape of her neck, a simplicity of style which suited
her regular features and showed the perfect shape of her
skull. Good bone structure, Max had said, and she
thought he would approve. Harry had disliked classical
effects, he had always wanted her to have her hair curled.
She, who had much better taste than he had done, had
refused, saying it would make her look like a barmaid.
What Harry had really meant was that he wanted her to
look more accessible. She definitely did not want to
appear accessible to Max.

Finally she applied a suspicion of eye-shadow to increase the lustre of her eyes, and colour to her lips. This done, she studied herself curiously. Two years ago, she had often made grand toilettes before a public appearance. On the night of her last concert, she had worn dark crimson velvet. A slight shiver ran through her as she recalled it. It had been prophetic to wear the colour of blood. Then she had been an eager young girl, anticipating success and fulfilment of love. Now she had become a woman, her anticipations unfulfilled. A faint aura of tragedy still lingered about her, reflected in the depths of her eyes, investing her with a hint of mystery.

The innocent candour of Sophy's still childish face rose before her mental vision, and she smiled a little bleakly. Sophy was still so young, and because of her infirmity, sheltered. Though the gap in years could not be great, she made Evelyn feel old and mature.

She did not attempt to conceal from herself that the goal of her efforts was to impress Max. She wanted him to see her as she had been in her glory and to carry away with him to distant Vienna, a glamorous memory. Beyond that she did not think. They had to part, that was inevitable, and for Sophy's sake they must behave circumspectly, but she hoped that after tonight, Max would leave her with a touch of regret, and not the relief, which she feared he might be beginning to feel.

He was calling for her early, because he was to give her a meal in Munich before the concert, as it was too soon to dine before they left. Evelyn was looking forward to the evening. It was the first time she had anticipated anything with pleasure for two long years. Excitement added a glow to her whole being. It was the prospect of hearing music again which was thrilling her, but had she been honest she would have had to admit that the thought of spending a long evening alone with Max was adding considerably to her expectations.

Amy was resting in her room, and Evelyn did not disturb her, knowing that her aunt thoroughly disapproved of this outing, and would disapprove even more, if she saw Evelyn's new dress.

Meaning to wait for Max in the lounge, she had descended half-way down the stairs, when the two children burst in from outside, and stopped to stare at her in amazement. Then recognizing her, Bobby exclaimed:

'Coo – it's the ghost!'

'She's not a ghost now, she shines,' Jane announced.

Evelyn looked at the two youthful faces turned upwards to her with amusement tinged with gratification. This reception of her changed appearance augured well for Max's reaction. She descended another two steps, saying:

'Why do you call me a ghost?'

' 'Cos you're always in black and white and faded-looking,' Bobby said candidly.

'Ssh!' Jane looked shocked. 'Mummy said you mustn't say that to her, it's rude, and she's been so kind, giving us presents.' She looked up at Evelyn anxiously. 'You're not angry?'

'No. Do you like my new dress?'

She was absurdly anxious for these small people's approbation, their assurance that she was not looking faded now.

Bobby had already lost interest and was looking around for another diversion, but Jane said fervently:

'It's lovely. When I'm a big lady I want one just like it. I love long dresses, but mine are all short or I have to wear trousers.'

'You'd look a sight in a long dress,' Bobby jeered with

brotherly candour.

Jane's little face puckered. 'You're horrid! I wouldn't, would I?'

'Of course not, but they aren't fashionable for little girls just now,' Evelyn told her diplomatically. 'You'll be able to have one when you're older.' Adding as she addressed Bobby, 'How's the German coming along?'

'Not very well, *danke schön*,' Bobby said despondently, but the reminder turned his thoughts in another direction. 'Is the lolly man coming?' he asked hopefully.

'Yes, but there won't be any lolly distribution tonight,' Evelyn said hastily.

'Does he give you lots of lollies?' Jane asked wistfully.

'Don't be silly,' her brother told her. 'Men don't give ladies lollies, they give 'em flowers. Will he bring you flowers?'

'We're going to a concert, and flowers would be in the way,' Evelyn pointed out.

'I like concerts,' Bobby announced, 'specially when there's a funny man. Couldn't you ask the lolly man to take us too?'

'I'm sure he would,' Jane added hopefully, 'he's ever so nice, he likes children.'

Evelyn thought Max might find the pair a little embarrassing, but there was one sure method of getting them out of the way, even though it might be a little unethical. She opened her bag.

'Is that gold?' Jane asked, round-eyed.

'No, not really.' Evelyn took out a note. 'Are the shops still open?'

'The café is ... Oh, is that for us?' Bobby clutched her offering ecstatically. 'I'm sorry I said you were a ghost, you don't look a bit like one now. Come on, Jane!'

They nearly collided with Max coming in, but having obtained their booty they were no longer interested in him. Evelyn saw that he was wearing a dinner jacket and realized that the concert would be a formal affair. She was thankful that she had bought the dress.

Max in evening clothes was impressive. His garments were perfectly cut and he was impeccably groomed. Fleetingly she again wondered who and what he was, for he could have passed for one of the Grand Dukes of the old régime.

He saw her standing on the lowest step of the stairs, her golden dress glimmering against the shadows behind her, and for a moment he stood stock still just within the front door, staring while a slow fire kindled in his eyes.

Evelyn completed her descent and dropped him a curtsey.

'Will I do?'

He came forward, clicked his heels together and bowed with exaggerated courtesy.

'Most radiant, exquisite and unmatchable beauty,' he quoted, and she laughed a little mockingly.

'*Twelfth Night*, and Viola didn't mean it.'

'No, but Orsino wrote the letter and he did, and so do I. He also said, "If music be the food of love, play on." We are going to have music tonight, Eve.'

'But we've no love that needs nourishing,' she said lightly, while her heartbeats increased their tempo. If she learned to love this man, and she feared she was doing so all too quickly, her love must be starved – and fast. 'Where did you learn your Shakespeare?' For this was the second time he had quoted from the bard.

'I have always liked the famous William and I think he is more appreciated abroad than he is at home. I have an idea that at one time the Germans claimed him as their own, inventing a new pedigree to prove his Teutonic descent.'

Voices above them and from outside heralded other guests arriving. Max offered her his arm.

'Come, let us be on our way.'

She laid her gloved hand upon his arm and her excitement grew.

'I've a feeling this is going to be a memorable night,' she said recklessly.

He turned his head to gaze down into her eyes with such a penetrating look that her heart missed a beat as she met their vivid blue.

'I sincerely hope it will be,' he said gravely.

Evelyn tried to withdraw her hand, assailed by a sudden panic. She ought not to go, she was being crazy. Music and Max was a combination with which she could not cope. But Max pressed her hand close to his side and swept her out on to the terrace. As if sensing her misgivings, he said firmly:

'It is much too late to turn back.'

Submissively she let him lead her to his car. She had not really wanted to return.

The road north to the frontier led through Scharnitz and the Porta Claudia, with the Wetterstein peaks on one side and the Karwendel on the other. At Scharnizt there was a particularly fine example of a mural painting on the side of a house. Evelyn suggested that some British houses might be improved by a little similar decoration, and amused herself inventing suitable pictures for various houses which she knew, assisted by suggestions from Max. The plain whitewashed vicarage in Amy's home village would be much enlivened by a row of haloed saints like some that she had seen in Austria. They both became very gay.

Max took the road through Garmisch Partenkirchen with the Zugspitze, the highest mountain in Germany, flanking their left. Then gradually the mountains fell behind them and they gained the motorway, speeding through mile upon mile of pretty wooded country, which seemed a little tame after the Alps.

As their destination neared, their gaiety faded into silence. Evelyn's apprehensions were returning, as she wondered if she were about to test her endurance too severely. She had attended many musical functions when she was not playing herself, usually with one of her teachers, never with Harry, who found what he termed 'highbrow' music boring. That this meant that a whole range of her thoughts and feelings were entirely divorced from him had not seemed important in the flush of their young love. So she would have no memories of Harry to disturb her, but music had always affected her emotions strongly. It would be terribly embarrassing if she lost control of herself. Max had already had to contend with her weeping and her faint, he would not appreciate having to do so again for what would seem to him to be no cause whatever.

Max too had become preoccupied and the set of his mouth was a little grim. Evelyn had no idea that he was fully aware of the ordeal through which she was about to pass, nor did she suspect that he had a motive for inflicting it upon her.

The outskirts of the town began to envelop them. They were much like those of any other capital city. Max broke his silence to observe:

'Like most towns, the only interesting part of Munich is the old part, and that is shrinking. How I hate these uniform erections of flats!'

'Is it the same in Vienna?'

'Unfortunately, yes.'

'Do you live in one?'

'No. I am fortunate. My mother and I inhabit an old house which my father left to us. It is rather a rambling old place, but it is lovely, and it is a real home. When I marry, I expect Mother will prefer to move into a modern flat. Elderly people care more for comfort and convenience than the picturesque.'

So when he married Sophy, he would install her in his family home, and if Sophy regained her sight, she would appreciate a house which was a home. Evelyn's spirits began to sink, but resolutely she sought to revive them. Max had asked her to accompany him to provide cheerful company to relieve the tedium of the long drive, and she was not playing her part. She would not let thoughts of Sophy intrude upon this evening. This was her night, and she did not think Sophy would be so ungenerous as to grudge it to her.

Thus when Max took her to dinner at a small, select restaurant, she endeavoured to chatter brightly about indifferent subjects and little by little her apprehensions and depression vanished. Max could be very good company and he could make her laugh. Munich, he told her, was more famed for its beer than music, and she ought to sample some.

She refused firmly, she did not like beer.

'And I don't want another of your special concoctions, either,' she said mischievously. 'I want to keep my head clear tonight.'

By referring to the evening of the dance, she hoped to shame him, but he only laughed and suggested sherry. He too, she concluded, meant to avoid emotional pitfalls tonight.

The concert hall was an old building, oval in shape, with a circle which housed the elite, the floor being filled with students in motley garb, who looked as though they might prove unruly, but when the music began, they became still as stone.

Whether by accident or design, Max arrived a little late. The orchestra was tuning up as he and Evelyn were shown into their seats at the end of the circle, where they had no one behind them and no one in front. They had a slightly one-sided view of the platform, but the piano was within their range. Spotlights illuminated it and the lights in the auditorium were subdued.

Evelyn was filled with almost unbearable nostalgia, as she saw the familiar scene, heard the whine of bows drawn across stringed instruments, a hoot from the brass. Then the conductor stepped on to the rostrum and raised his baton. The first part of the programme was devoted to Mozart, and as the familiar strains reached her, Evelyn lost all consciousness of her own identity. She listened not only with her ears, but her whole body; she was, as it were, inside the music, every fibre of her being vibrating to each note, while her spirit soared into a celestial sphere.

Hans Schreiberg played a solo, the sonata in C Minor. He was a thin, pale young man with black locks of hair falling over his face. He played with absolute precision. but there was something empty about his performance; it was intellectual more than emotional; when emotion was needed, it was applied, not felt. But Evelyn was too moved by her own sensations to be critical. Not so Max.

'He plays with his head but has forgotten his heart,' was his comment.

Evelyn did not hear him; she was not even conscious of his presence beside her.

During the interval, she was still enveloped in the aura

of the music. Max glanced at her rapt face, but made no comment. Again she did not hear him when he offered her refreshment, nor his murmured excuse that he had to speak to someone. He slipped away and left her completely lost to her surroundings.

During the second half it was different, for this was devoted to the work of Franz Liszt.

In three of the Hungarian Rhapsodies, where pianism is the principal concern. Schreiberg was again performing, and Evelyn became restless. Again his performance lacked depth and he made up for his deficiencies with an obvious display which imposed a false image upon the compositions, romanticizing them with a cheapening effect. Her pure taste was offended. She glanced at Max and saw he was watching young Hans with a satirical twist of his lip. Catching her eye, he smiled with understanding and her heart leaped to realize that musically they were in complete accord.

The climax came when Schreiberg attempted the 'Totentanz'. This had been the last work that Evelyn had ever played, and something sombre in the depths of her nature, perhaps some presage of the doom to come, had enabled her to impart to it a breadth of demonic power and almost Satanic intensity. In her hands it had been chillingly macabre, but Schreiberg played it in a hectic rush, trying to convey by speed what he failed to do by interpretation.

Evelyn's appreciation changed to violent irritation. If only it had been within her power to show him how it should be played!

'I can't bear it,' she whispered. 'It's awful!' Her voice rose hysterically: 'He can't play it, it's murder!'

'Ssh!' whispered their neighbours.

Her gloved hands went to her throat, as if she were

choking. 'And I can't either . . . now!'

Max's arm about her waist . . . Max leading her away as inconspicuously as possible.

'The lady is not well,' he said to the usher, who was looking daggers at them for the interruption.

He took her into the refreshment room behind the circle. It was deserted and in half darkness, its customers having gone back into the hall after the interval. Only in one distant corner two men were finding business more interesting than music. They did not even look up when Evelyn and Max came in. He put her in a chair with her back to the room and went to the counter to fetch coffee for her. The attendant glanced at her indifferently. From the hall distant strains of music penetrated the silence like silver threads. Evelyn shuddered.

Max set the coffee before her, his face grave and intent. Becoming aware of his presence, she looked up with an apologetic smile.

'I'm so sorry . . . but I couldn't bear it.'

He sat down beside her, taking her left hand in his.

'Tell me,' he said insistently.

She looked at him vaguely, as if he were a stranger.

'You see, I played that piece once,' she whispered. A little proud smile curved her lips. 'But I played it as it should be played.'

'I know. I heard you.'

His words penetrated her numbed brain. She straightened herself in her chair and her eyes widened with incredulity.

'You couldn't have done!'

'But I did. I went to London to hear Evelina Ravelli.'

'Then . . . then you know everything?'

'I think I have pieced the story together.' Very gently

123

he lifted her hand and touched each fingertip with his lips. 'Was there no miracle for this?'

'No, miracles don't happen to people like me.' She snatched her hand away. If ever she had told him about her lost career, she had meant it to be a dramatic revelation, not a whispered confession in a coffee bar, but there was nothing to reveal. If he had seen her in London, he must have known from the start who she was.

'Then ... when you met me on the *alm* ... you recognized me?'

'I thought I did, but I was not sure. The name was different, but the initials were the same. I always suspected Evelina Ravelli was a pseudonym, it was a little ... unlikely; besides, you had changed.'

'Do you wonder?' she cried wildly. 'Do you wonder?'

'Hush, Eve,' he said sternly, as one of the businessmen raised an inquiring head. 'Drink your coffee.'

She obeyed and gradually her agitation subsided to be replaced by curiosity.

'But why did you come to hear me? I don't suppose my name was known in Austria ... though it might have been if ...' She swallowed convulsively.

'Music is my business. I have a controlling interest in several concert halls. I had heard reports of you, reports which I must admit I was ready to discount. I had other business in London, so I took the opportunity of coming to hear you. I expected to find the usual talented young lady, but I found a genius. I also found ... something else.'

Only two words registered. 'You thought I had genius? Really?'

'As far as a pianist can be a genius, yes. Liszt himself could not have played better than you did.'

'Oh!' Her eyes fell on her left hand. 'And then this had to happen,' she said, moving the feeble fingers.

'There are other things which you could do,' he suggested, ignoring the desperation in her voice. 'Have you never tried to compose?'

'Oh yes, silly childish things. I'm not a composer, I'm an interpreter.'

'But you have music in your soul. It might have been a compensation.'

'Nothing could compensate,' she told him passionately. 'Do you think I would want to be a third-rate composer when I had been a first-grade pianist? I want the best, or nothing.'

'I see your point.'

'But you . . . you're a musician too?' she asked wonderingly. 'Do you compose?'

'No. I play various instruments, but not professionally. I conduct upon occasion. Music means a great deal to me.'

'Yet you gave me no hint until yesterday?'

'I was given to understand music was a sore subject with you,' he said dryly, 'and when I risked asking you to come with me tonight, and you fainted, I thought I really had thrown the fat on the fire.'

'Poor Max!' She laughed a little shamefacedly. 'But I'm awfully glad you did, you've broken the hoodoo.'

'Which was what I hoped to do.'

'You must think I'm an idiotic sort of creature,' she said sadly, 'with all my inhibitions. But I wasn't always so.' She looked at him thoughtfully, wishing that he could have known her in her prime. 'You were impressed by my playing, so if fate had been kinder we would have met anyhow, but in very different circumstances, and I shouldn't have been a weeping ghost.' She sighed for the might-have-been. She would have been a radiant star. 'When I saw your hand I began to put two and two together. I had been trying to find Evelina Ravelli for a long time. I had expected there would be other concerts, that, like a comet, you would blaze your way through Europe, but when there was no further mention of you, I began to think something must have happened to you. Your agent said he knew nothing, and I was intensely disappointed when all my efforts to trace you failed.'

'Why? I wasn't so very important.'

'You were to me,' he said simply. Then noticing the dubious look on her face, he laughed and added: 'Naturally I wanted to sign you up before your fees became too exorbitant. But how did you manage to muzzle the Press? As far as I know, your accident was never reported, or I should have seen it.'

'Oh, but it was, complete with a photograph of Harry. He was the risen star. I was only rising. Very few people knew my real name and the gossip columnists hadn't got round to probing into my private life. I wasn't even seriously injured.' She smiled wryly. 'I think I was just mentioned as Harry's fiancée. He would have preferred it, that way, he always said one celebrity in a family was enough.'

'But his sport could not be compared with your art.'

'Exactly. Harry had no use for art and I was going to give up playing in public when we were married.'

'He would have allowed you to do that?'

'He wanted me to.'

'*Du liebe Gott!* The man must have been mad! Did he not know that talent like yours is born once in a generation?'

'He was a sportsman, he found serious music dull.'

'You must have been mad too to think of marrying him.' Evelyn's eyes sparkled dangerously, but he went on heedlessly. 'I can understand how you felt when you were deprived of your piano, but I cannot understand your infatuation for a singularly worthless man. The injury to your hand caused an irreplaceable loss to the world, but your sentimental clinging to Harry Travers' memory made me very angry.'

'I grasped that, I'm not entirely dim,' Evelyn returned, 'but I was mourning for my music too. I hoped you would never discover who I had been, when I had become such a travesty of myself.'

'That made me even more angry, it was so unnecessary. You are so beautiful, Eve. and you persisted in trying to make a fright of yourself.'

The warmth in look and voice softened her, though she was indignant about the outrageous things he had been saying.

'Well, I'm not a fright tonight, am I?' she asked, but omitted to mention that she had dressed up solely to please him.

'Far from it, and I hope you have finally discarded your uniform of woe.'

'But I really did love Harry,' she insisted, 'and it wasn't very nice of you to give him away to Aunt Amy.'

'She knew,' he said shortly, 'everyone knew except you. The person most concerned is always the last to know. I hope the disclosure finally killed your love.'

The revelation had arrived much too late to really hurt her, for her love had faded far away into the past, but she was not going to admit that to Max. She had to have some bulwark against Sophy. It was plain to her that his interest had been solely in Evelina, he had admired her talent and apparently also her face. Shocked by the wreck which she had become, he had sought to revitalize her and tonight his work was completed – he had brought her back to music, and she would never deny it again.

'You can't kill love,' she told him. 'Although he was faithless, I shall always love Harry.'

Her statement was partly true. Harry had been her young dream. She would always look back upon that period of her life with nostalgia, as much for her own happy girlhood as for him.

But her statement had evidently displeased Max, for he was frowning heavily.

'Do you want to hear any more of the concert?' he asked abruptly.

'Do you want to?' she inquired politely.

'No, my purpose is accomplished.'

So he had engineered the outing to make her give herself away. A very devious man, she thought bitterly; he could easily have told her he knew who she was without dragging her to Munich. But would she have transformed herself without the stimulus of the anticipated concert, in fact, would she have emerged from her shell at all without his guiding hand? He was too diabolically clever, manipulating her like a puppet, but it was not strings he pulled, it was emotions.

'Then if you really don't mind, I would prefer not to hear any more,' she told him. 'If I'm to live with music again, I can only take it in small doses to begin with.'

'*Sehr gut*, we will then go back.'

He still seemed annoyed.

'Haven't I reacted in the way you hoped?' she asked sweetly.

He smiled sardonically. 'Not entirely.'

'Ah, but women are supposed to be unpredictable, aren't they?'

'That is part of their charm.' But he did not look as if he were finding her charming.

As they descended to the vestibule, a big bearded man

128

came hurrying out of the hall. Seeing Max, he rushed up to him, embracing him boisterously.

'Max! *Mein freund!*' and he deluged him with a torrent of German.

When he paused for breath, Max said in English:

'I know I have overstayed my leave, but I will soon be back and the matter can wait. But what brings you here?'

'I come to hear the young Schreiberg! His eyes twinkled under his bushy brows. 'Is he not *wunderbar*? Do you not bust yourself to engage him?'

'I do not,' Max said decidedly.

The other man laughed uproariously. *'Gut! Gut!'* He stopped and looked sad. 'The good pianists, where have they gone?' His eyes fell upon Evelyn. He stared at her with slowing dawning recognition.

'But this is really *wunderbar*! My good friend, you have found her at last! Fräulein Ravelli, you will come to Wien? You will play for us? Max, I forgive you for your delay now I know its cause. We will show this Schreiberg what good playing is, *nicht wahr?'*

He turned back to Max, and muttered in German, 'Is she very expensive?'

For Evelyn it was a bitter moment. Passionately she wished it was within her power to do what she was asked, but it was not. All the wishing in the world would not give her back the strength in her left hand.

'You are mistaken, *Mein Herr . . .'* she faltered, and looked appealingly at Max.'

Max said something vehement to his friend in German and the man looked bewildered.

'Ich verstehte nicht,' he muttered.

Max took Evelyn's arm and hurried her away.

'That blundering ass was Herr Schmitt,' he said between his teeth, 'he came with me to London to hear you play. Unfortunately he recognized you.'

Evelyn's eyes were full of the old sombre brooding.

'You see now why I wanted to hide myself away,' she said painfully.

He said nothing to that, but hastily stowed her into his car. They were some way out of Munich before he discovered that she was crying, softly, hopelessly and without sound.

'Eve, please do not do that,' he besought her distractedly.

With an effort she controlled her tears.

'I suppose it didn't occur to you,' she said in a muffled voice, 'before you embarked upon your rescue act, that I might prefer to remain as I was.'

'Would you really prefer to be miserable, for you were miserable, Eve, and make everyone around you miserable too?' He spoke almost savagely. 'I wanted to make you happier.'

'It wasn't your affair,' she said drearily. 'You had no right to interfere.'

'If I saw a drowning man, should I not try to save him?'

'But I wasn't drowning. I think you've missed your vocation, Max. You should have been a doctor, not a musician.'

His brows knitted in puzzlement. 'A doctor, because I wanted to help you?'

'And try out your own peculiar brand of therapy, which even included kissing me.' She laughed a little wildly and saw his hands tighten on the steering wheel. 'You make a speciality of lame ducks, don't you?'

'Lame ducks? What do you mean?'

'The halt and the blind, me and Sophy.'

'Ah, poor Sophy,' he sighed. His thoughts diverted, he relaxed. 'Her ordeal will soon be upon her. I think of her almost hourly.'

This information increased Evelyn's feeling of bitter frustration. If Max's concern for herself had been motivated by love, how very different the situation would be. She would then have so gladly leaned upon him, given herself and her life into his keeping and been happy.

'She'll have you there to hold her hand,' she reminded him.

'*Ach so*, I hope I can be of help to her.'

'I'm sure you will be, you're so good at it.' And now her sarcasm was obvious.

'What would you have me do?' he asked in a puzzled tone. 'I have known Sophy all her life, she means a great deal to me. It is mainly owing to my persuasions that she is undergoing this operation, and if that fails too . . .' He left the sentence unfinished.

'You'll be able to console her, I'm sure,' Evelyn said harshly. 'Who is your other failure?'

'Yourself.'

'That must distress you greatly. So much effort expended for nothing. Perhaps you'd like to try kissing me again, while I'm still looking glamorous? Before Cinderella returns to her rags.'

'Eve, you cannot!' He sounded appalled by the implication of her words.

'Oh yes, I can. You didn't think you had effected a permanent cure, did you? It would take a cleverer man than you to do that, Max Linden, and one who was unattached.'

She was intent upon provoking him. She had suffered too many emotions during the evening – eager anticipation, the profound feeling music always stirred in her, the agony of loss which Herr Schmitt's blundering had reawakened, which was intensified by the reminder that Max was going back to Vienna, that Sophy occupied his tenderest thoughts, and she would be left with nothing to sustain her.

'What the hell do you mean?' he asked angrily.

'You know what I mean. But I'm not entirely negligible, am I? You didn't exactly dislike kissing me on the Karer. Why don't you do it again while you have the chance? It will give us both something to remember when . . . when . . .' She was going to say, 'We're far apart,' but the words stuck in her throat.

Max swore softly under his breath and accelerated.

A growing desire for his kiss drove Evelyn to further madness. It was little enough to take with her into the black and lonely future ahead of her. If she could only for a few moments assuage her sore heart in his arms, she would not be harming Sophy. Sophy need never know, and she would have Max for the rest of her life. But Max seemed impervious to her invitation. He was thinking only of his beloved.

Goaded beyond endurance, she said sweetly: 'I thought I was looking rather better than I did up on the Karer, but it seems your ardour has cooled.'

'*Du liebe Gott*,' he said between his teeth. 'You are wrong there, my girl, but only an imbecile would make overtures to a man on a motorway.'

She had forgotten that he could not stop.

'I am looking for a pull-in,' he went on ominously, 'and then I will show you.'

A chill crept down Evelyn's spine. She had been crazy to try to provoke him, and he was going to take her at her word.

'I . . . I only suggested you might kiss me,' she said

hurriedly, 'as . . . as a reward for taking me out. It's usual, isn't it?'

'Usual or not, it is what I am going to do,' he returned.

A side turning appeared and he slewed off the motorway. The car bumped on the verge, the engine died, and he switched off the lights. There was little traffic about and the night was very still. A low moon hung in the sky above the dark woods which bordered the fields, surprising in one of them, a gleam of water.

She heard a click as Max released his safety belt, and he turned towards her. It was too dark to see his face, but he looked menacing. He made an abrupt movement towards her, and caught his elbow on the steering wheel. Again he swore.

'Definitely not the time and place,' Evelyn said a little shakily. 'We . . . we'd better postpone it.'

'Will we, hell!'

He took her then in an embrace which had no hint of tenderness. Evelyn's blood leaped in response. Fear, bitterness and despair were blotted out as their banked fires were released. She yielded her body and her lips, and her loosened hair covered them both like a veil. She knew then that love had been born in her again and both body and soul yearned towards Sophy's man.

Suddenly Max released his hold of her, letting her sink back into her seat. He unwound the window beside him, allowing the cool night air to blow into the car. Taking out his handkerchief, he wiped his forehead.

'Forgive me for being rough,' he muttered unsteadily. 'You drove me mad.'

She wanted to cry out that she loved his madness, that there was nothing she would not do for him, but pride and prudence restrained her. If she were ready to give all for love, he was only seeking a temporary gratification.

Then he did a surprising thing. He picked up a lock of her hair and kissed it almost with reverence. He let it fall and pulled out the starter.

'It is time we were getting on,' he said huskily. 'Fasten your seat belt.'

In silence Evelyn fumbled with the straps. She had had her moment. Max would leave her, as Harry had left her, in a vacuum.

Max had to make a wide detour to get back on to the motorway. He relieved his feelings by fulminating about its design during this operation.

'Excellent for getting from A to Z,' he grumbled, 'but the devil if one deviates.'

'Like most things in life,' Evelyn said, 'there are always difficulties if one leaves the straight path.'

'Very profound,' he almost sneered. 'And where do you propose to go from here?'

'Nowhere,' she said quietly. 'The episode is closed.'

Suddenly everything became very clear. Loving Max, she would not fail him. What he had begun, she would complete.

'You will go back to Vienna,' she went on, 'and I shall go back to England. I know I behaved bitchily tonight, but I'm going to be a good girl from now on.' She smiled infinitely sadly, a smile it was too dark for him to see. 'But I'm not going to revert to my bad old ways. I only said that to . . . to provoke you. I shall find something useful to do and stop pitying myself. As you've told me before, there are others worse off than I am. But I'll never forget you, Max, you have helped me, though I know I haven't been very nice about it. I . . . I really am grateful to you.'

'*Danke Gott*,' he said so devoutly that Evelyn was

startled. 'But why do you talk about parting? After to-night surely that is impossible?'

A wave of triumph surged over her. He had completely forgotten Sophy, but it was a barren triumph, for there could be no future for her with him. Even if she could, she was not so mean as to take him from Sophy, and he could not seriously be thinking of jilting her.

'It would be better for us to part,' she said stonily.

'But, *liebchen,* do not you love me?'

Then she understood. By her crazy conduct she had aroused expectations which she could not fulfil. Believing that she loved him, he thought she would be prepared to have an affair with him while he waited for Sophy to recover from her operation. She was disappointed, for she had not thought Max was so cynical, but he was a foreigner with a continental outlook, and a musician's temperament, which though it did not excuse him, explained him.

There was only one way to keep him at arm's length, for she could not trust herself if he attempted physical persuasion. She would have to deny her love.

'No,' she said, 'I don't.'

'You responded as if you did.'

'Oh, that – a biological reflex, I suppose. I'm sorry, Max, the music excited me, it made me a little mad. I hardly knew what I was doing, but now I'm sane again.'

'Is it still Harry?' he asked.

She seized upon the pretext he offered.

'Well, yes, I suppose it is. You see, I know what real love is. I'll never feel for any other man what I did for him.'

And that, she thought, was in a sense true. Her love for Max was of a different quality from what she had felt for

Harry, deeper, more mature. Harry had been the hero of her girlish dreams, he had epitomized romance. Possibly she had actually been more in love with love than the man himself.

'It is surprising how women can love a rake,' Max said bitterly.

But Max was no better himself. Pledged to one girl, he was ready to deceive her with another, exactly what Harry had done.

The accusation was on the tip of her tongue, but she did not utter it. To what end? she thought wearily. He was keen for her now, he might even deny that he loved Sophy. Men lost their heads when they were in the grip of desire, but he would go back to Sophy; he knew she needed his support.

They had left the motorway and were passing through Garmisch Partenkirchen. The streets were deserted, and she realized it was very late. The Zugspitze rose before them, black and formidable against the moonlit sky.

'Can't you go a little faster?' she asked. 'Aunt Amy may worry if I'm very late.'

Max gave a long sigh. 'But Eve, *mein hertz, mein leben*, Harry is dead.'

'I know, you don't have to remind me of that,' she said sharply. Turning her face to the window, she surreptitiously wiped from her eyes the tears that had risen to them, not tears for Harry, but tears because she must lose Max.

Max drove even more slowly to negotiate a tricky bend. He turned and looked at her. 'So, *liebchen*, I am to understand that you do not want me?'

Dumbly she shook her head. She was yearning for him.

'But I may still be your friend?'

'If you wish.'

A dangerous friendship, but it would not be for long, he would be going back to Vienna and Sophy.

'*Ach so*, and while there's life there's hope.' He spoke almost cheerfully, and at last began to accelerate. The car sped towards Scharnitz.

But what was there to hope for?

Presently he said:

'We have not much further to go, you had better do something about your hair.'

'But who's to see?' she exclaimed.

'The frontier,' he reminded her.

She had completely forgotten that they would be stopped and inspected. Hastily she began to braid her locks and tidy her dress.

'I should hate the guard to think ... what they might think,' Max said slyly.

Evelyn blushed in the dark.

'That I'm an abandoned woman?' she asked. 'I nearly was, you know.'

'If only you had been a little more so,' he sighed, 'but I must be content with what I was given.'

Steeling herself against the regret in his voice, Evelyn said brazenly, 'I've often wondered how one set about seducing a man. It's much easier than I thought.' She strove to keep her voice flippant.

'But do not make a habit of it,' he warned her. 'The next one might not know when to stop.'

Light words, spoken jestingly, but with a dagger-sharp edge. The next one? Was he prepared to surrender her so easily? It meant nothing to him, in spite of his protestations that other men might kiss her. After her behaviour tonight he would expect that they would and he felt no jealousy.

But there would not be a next time.

CHAPTER SEVEN

BESIDE Evelyn's bed there was again a little pot of wild flowers, but they were neither an offering to Harry nor a gift from Max.

When Evelyn had arrived back, she was so late that she was the last person to enter the hotel, and Amy was sound asleep. Propped against her bedroom door she had found the bunch of wild flowers and a piece of grubby paper inscribed with sprawling capitals:

WE PIK THESE FOR YOU. BOBBY AND JANE.

The little attention had pleased her and she had carefully put the wilting bouquet in water before she undressed.

The evening had become a kaleidoscope of whirling impressions, but she was too exhausted to feel any more emotion. She slept at once.

She woke to the recollection that today they were to go to visit the Hartmanns, and the prospect was unwelcome. Max was taking them and she would have to spend several hours with him and Sophy. Knowing now that she loved him herself, it would be painful to watch that display of tender adoration which he reserved for Sophy alone. Sophy's lover and the Max she knew were like two different people. Sophy appealed to the best in him, while she seemed to bring out the worst. But she had behaved abominably last night, so it was hardly fair to blame him for following her lead. It had certainly been a night to remember, and she felt a stir of resentment against Max when she began to sort out the details. He was continuing to treat her like a specimen under a glass dome, whose behaviour pattern changed under varying stimuli, and the visit to Munich had been another experiment. No doubt he had been intrigued when he found Evelina Ravelli weeping on a mountainside, whom he had last seen in all the glory of her success. That had incited him to use all his charm and determination to break through her atrophy, and it must have been so very flattering to his vanity to discover she was responding to him when no one else had been able to make any impact. The climax had come last night, when she had certainly given him a run for his money. The specimen had escaped from its glass dome and become a human being, demanding recompense for being analysed, but she had baulked at the final capitulation. Galatea fell in love with her creator, Pygmalion, but she had refused to award to Max that final triumph. Dead Harry had saved her from the humiliation of confessing that she loved where no love was.

She had made him believe that he had not succeeded in obliterating Harry's memory, and he would not, she decided, make any further advance. Time was running out, he had to return to his duties. Herr Schmitt had indicated that he had already overstayed his leave, and Sophy would need all his care and attention. She wished that she need not see Sophy today. She did not feel exactly guilty, she had after all kept Max faithful to his fiancée, but the meeting would not be without embarrassment.

Amy came in while she was dressing to inquire about the evening's entertainment and apologized for not sitting up for her.

'You were so very late,' she said reproachfully.

'It's a long way,' Evelyn reminded her. She was sitting at her dressing table, brushing her hair. Sweeping it back, she looked at her aunt accusingly:

'When did Max tell you he knew I was Evelina Ravelli?'

Amy looked taken aback. 'Has he found out?'

'Don't pretend. It was when we came back from the dance, wasn't it?'

'My dear, of course he'd recognized you. All I wanted to do was to warn him to be careful what he said to you . . .'

'And you knew who he was, but you didn't tell me?'

'You are . . . were not very receptive to reminders about the past,' Amy said with spirit.

Evelyn laughed. 'Poor Auntie, I'm afraid I've been quite unbearable, but from now on you needn't try to shield me any more. I've come to terms with the past and I'm going to behave like a normal person, and I'm very, very grateful to you for all your forbearance, this lovely holiday and . . . everything!'

She stood up and kissed her aunt.

'Oh, darling, I'm so thankful . . .'

'Please, Auntie, say no more about it, and it must be time for breakfast.'

As she came down into the dining-room, Evelyn's thoughts reverted to Sophy. Looking round at the very ordinary people assembled there, she wondered what would be Sophy's impression of the human race, which she had never clearly seen before. For the most part it appeared uncommonly plain, she thought ruefully, and if Sophy expected everyone to be beautiful, she was going to be disillusioned. Then her eyes went to the lovely day outside the window. Nature was always beautiful, and Sophy would have the loveliest thing of all, light.

Bobby and Jane were looking at her expectantly, and she crossed to their table to thank them for the flowers.

'It was a nice thought,' she told them.

The children looked gratified.

'You was so pretty,' Jane said. 'Why you not always wear that dress?'

'It's hardly suitable for the daytime.'

'I've heard so much about what you wore last night,' Mrs. Lambert said, 'it seems to have made a great impression upon Jane. Must have been quite something.'

'All gold and glowing,' Jane nodded.

'I expect the colour took her fancy,' Evelyn suggested. This morning she was in white, her trousers having returned from the cleaners, and she wondered if Bobby thought she was a ghost again. She doubted if she would ever wear the golden dress again, and all the glow had faded.

Max arrived during the morning to arrange what time he was to collect them in the afternoon. Evelyn was playing ball with the children, and as he came without the car, she did not notice he was standing watching her, with satisfaction upon his face, until Bobby cried:

'There's the lolly man. Catch!' and threw the ball to him.

Max caught it adroitly in one hand, and Jane applauded. He threw it gently towards her so that she could catch it, but it slipped from her grasp.

'Butterfingers!' Bobby jeered.

Jane looked crestfallen, but Evelyn picked up the ball and threw it with such care that this time the child managed to hold it.

'Throw it to me!' Bobby yelled impatiently, hopping from one leg to the other, but Jane, smiling impishly, bestowed it upon Max.

She's beginning early, Evelyn thought, knowing that Max had made another conquest. She remembered that he had said he liked children. When he finally declared that he could play no more, and must discharge his errand, she said, as she preceded him up the steps,

'You seem to have a way with little ones.'

'I have nieces and nephews,' he explained, bringing home to her again how little she knew about him. 'I have a married sister living in Salzburg. She is a great friend of the Hartmanns.'

Sophy would be cognizant of all his connections, knew the sister and her children, she was not an outsider like Evelyn was. This afternoon was going to be difficult. Max was a cool hand, she decided, if he foresaw no embarrassment in their joint company. After all, he had embraced her very thoroughly last night, and she might be provoked into telling Sophy. The girl would be outraged and hurt. No, she could not tell Sophy anything, and Max knew that she would not.

She saw he was looking doubtfully at her clothes, and she said frankly: 'It will take a little time and expense to renovate my wardrobe.'

He registered faint surprise. Evidently it had not occurred to him that she was not in a position to rush out and buy whatever she wanted. Piano playing was not as lucrative as pop singing. Her father gave her an allowance, and her aunt was paying for their holiday, but upon her return she must find some means of earning something for herself.

Max continued to regard her thoughtfully and she wondered if he was assessing her means.

'I am, you see, out of a job,' she said bluntly, 'but I'm hoping to find something that I can do.'

'That should not be difficult,' he said carelessly, but his attention seemed to be wandering. Evelyn Rivers' employment problems could hardly be expected to interest him. They sat down on the cane chairs on the terrace.

'About this afternoon,' he began, 'I shall be delighted to drive you and your aunt in and out of Innsbruck, but I am afraid I shall not be able to stay with you. I have an unexpected engagement.'

So he was not as thick-skinned as she had supposed. He shrank from spending an afternoon with his two women in juxtaposition.

'The Hartmanns are friendly folk,' he went on, 'so I have no qualms about leaving you with them. They will make you feel at home.'

Evelyn was doubtful about that, but she was immensely relieved to learn that Max was going to absent himself. He told her that he had had an S O S to adjudicate at a local band competition, their man having let them down. Evelyn was surprised, surely such a proceeding was beneath him, but he explained that he had a very soft spot for the Tyrol and all its denizens, having been born there, and was always ready to subscribe to their local amusements.

'I think that's very nice of you,' Evelyn told him sincerely. 'They must feel highly honoured.'

'On the contrary, they think they are honouring me,' he said drily. 'I am only a Viennese musical director, but they are the elite musicians of the mountain villages.'

'Is that how they think of themselves?'

'Oh, very definitely.' He laughed. 'But I doubt if you would appreciate their performance.'

She would have very much preferred it to spending an afternoon with Sophy Hartmann, but that she dared not hint. He seemed to see nothing out of the way in taking her to visit his fiancée – for if they were not officially engaged, they were practically so – when only last night he had suggested a close relationship with herself. Perhaps she had misunderstood him, she had been in a very emotional state and her recollections were a little confused. There was nothing in his demeanour this morning to imply that theirs was anything more than a casual acquaintanceship.

Amy came out to join them and soon afterwards he took his leave. He had a lunch date, he told them, but he would be back in good time to collect them.

The way to Innsbruck was becoming familiar to Evelyn. There had been a shower at midday, the clouds obscuring the mountains, but when Max came to fetch them, faint gleams of sunshine were breaking through and their shapes began to emerge through the trailing scarves of mist. One by one the distant peaks would be revealed as the cloud shapes rolled away. The changing landscape had a fascination for Evelyn.

The Hartmanns' house was by the river on the outskirts of the town, and although not an old building, was constructed in the usual Alpine pattern with balconies running round outside the upstairs windows, and a great deal of woodwork in its upper structure. There was an extensive garden adorned with several weeping willows.

Herr Hartmann and his wife were a charming, friendly couple, and both spoke recognizable English. Sophy, wearing a flowered silk dress in blues and mauves, greeted them prettily, holding out both her little hands for Evelyn and Amy to take, which Evelyn did with some reluctance. It was impossible to dislike Sophy, but under the circumstances, she had no wish to become intimate with her.

When she had greeted them, Max came to her and taking a hand in each of his, raised them in turn to his lips.

They made a charming picture, the tall, blond man,

with the tender look on his strong face which Sophy always evoked, and the small, slim, golden-haired girl, but Evelyn could not appreciate it. Jealousy had descended upon her like a black cloud, shocking her with its intensity. She had to fight hard to reason herself out of it. It was not Sophy's fault that Max loved her, it was her good fortune and her compensation for her disability. But though her whole face expressed devotion, Evelyn found she was wondering if that fragile personality were capable of returning Max's passion. There was an air so essentially virginal about Sophy that it was difficult to imagine a man doing more than kiss her fingertips. She checked her thoughts sharply; they were engendered by jealousy, Sophy for all her puritan look was a normal girl and her inaccessibility would make her even more desirable to Max, who would know that, unlike herself, no other man had touched her.

'I am afraid I must go,' Max was saying, 'my competitors await my coming. This is only hail and farewell.'

'Perhaps ... Eva, is it not? ... to the competition would like to go?' Frau Hartmann suggested. 'We have not much of the entertainment to offer her.'

'Eva has come to see me,' Sophy said decidedly. 'Max, I am sure, can spare her to me for one day, and I do not wish to hear the bands, which I have heard many times before.'

Spoken tranquilly, but was there a faint hint of reproach in the vague blue eyes? Possibly Sophy was human enough to resent the expedition to the Brenner, and did she know about Munich? Evelyn caught a disconcerting gleam in Max's eyes, and was sure that she did not. She said quickly:

'Of course I'd prefer to stay with you, Sophy.'

145

'So that you can both dissect me between you?' Max asked mischievously.

'*Ach*, but you are vain!' Sophy told him. 'Do you think that we have nothing to talk of but of you? Be off with you to your task, and be sure we shall not mention you at all.'

Which Evelyn hoped would be true. She dreaded having to receive confidences about Max from Sophy.

Max laughed good-humouredly. '*Ach, so*, having had my ego deflated, I will bow my diminished head and take my leave. *Auf wiedersehen.*'

When he had gone Frau Hartmann complained that though he was on holiday, he took no rest.

'He lunch here, then go back to Seefeld and come again, now he rush off, then back again.'

'I'd no idea he came back specially to fetch us,' Amy exclaimed. 'We could have come in by train.'

Herr Hartmann smiled. '*Ach*, that could not be permitted.'

'Max wanted to see me about something very important,' Sophy explained. 'Eva, where are you? You shall come with me to my room and we will leave these old ones to their gossip, *nicht wahr?*'

'We will call you for tea,' her mother said.

Amid the familiar surroundings of her own home, Sophy's disability was not apparent. She knew exactly where every article, each piece of furniture was placed and how to gauge her distances. She led the way upstairs with confidence.

Her room was bare and functional, there were none of the trimmings with which a young girl likes to surround herself, and it brought home to Evelyn forcibly Sophy's limitations. Plain wood floor, walls and ceiling, the few strips of carpet securely fastened down, no pictures, books or looking glasses, and no bedside lamp. A transistor stood on the night table beside a bell. The only ornamentation was in one corner, where a prie-dieu was set before a crucifix hanging on the wall, and on the shelf below it were candles in carved candlesticks, with between them a bowl in which a dark-haired girl was arranging some early rosebuds. There was nothing unusual about this miniature oratory in a Catholic home, but it made Evelyn wonder if Sophy were very religious.

'*Grüss Gott, Fräulein,*' the girl said shyly.

'Anneliese, my devoted attendant,' Sophy introduced her.

Anneliese put in the last rosebud, dropped a curtsey and withdrew.

'She leave me to be married,' Sophy said with a sigh. 'Her loss will be very great.'

The windows were open to the balcony, through which poured the sun, which had won a final victory over the clouds. Sophy raised her face towards it.

'This room gets all the sun,' she said. 'The view, I am told, is pleasant, that I cannot see . . . yet . . . but I can feel the sun. You like my room? *Ja?*'

Evelyn said politely that it was lovely.

'Sit down somewhere,' Sophy bade her, waving a vague hand. 'The armchair is comfortable.'

This was upholstered and placed near the window, but while Evelyn seated herself, Sophy walked restlessly up and down.

'You know I am to go to hospital next week?' she asked. 'This doctor, he is very wise, very famous. I go to him some time back, he tell my father he can make me see.'

'That will be wonderful.'

Sophy's eyebrows puckered. 'So everyone tell me, but it

will be very strange . . .'

'Surely you cannot hesitate?'

'Max tells me I must have it done, and I want to be the normal person so I can gain my heart's desire. Max says it does not matter, but he is wrong. I cannot give myself unless I am whole. I would not wish to be taken out of pity.'

Sophy's idioms were at times a little difficult to follow, but to Evelyn it was plain that she had her pride, and she feared that Max's love for her was only pity. Upon that point Evelyn could reassure her, she had seen Max's face when he looked at Sophy.

'I'm sure Max adores you just because you are you.'

Sophy smiled tenderly. '*Ach*, dear Max! I have known him all my life and I have always leaned upon him, perhaps too much so, but whatever happens I know he will never fail me.' She sighed. 'I would like so much for him to be happy.'

'But he will be that if . . .' Eve hesitated; she had been going to say 'if you're cured', but Sophy might not be cured. She genuinely hoped she would be, since Max's happiness depended upon it. But Sophy's calm confidence in him was a little painful, though she would not have done anything to shake it. Only from her own experience of him, she had doubts. Though he adored Sophy, had he been faithful to her?

Sophy came towards Evelyn and touched her shoulder.

'May I touch your face?' she asked shyly. 'It is the only way in which I can judge what a person looks like.'

'If you wish,' Evelyn said gently.

The girl's small hand moved over Evelyn's face, lingering upon each feature, light as a butterfly's wing.

'It is a good face,' she said. 'Max has told me you have

known great pain and loss. He heard you play in London. He said you looked so beautiful.'

'I hoped it was my playing that impressed him,' Evelyn said a little dryly.

'That too. I have heard you play.'

'But you couldn't . . .'

'It was broadcast.'

'Yes, of course.' She had forgotten that. She had been recorded once or twice.

'Do not you love Max too?' Sophy asked insinuatingly.

The hot colour swept over Evelyn's face and she was thankful Sophy could not see it. Controlling her voice, she said steadily:

'My only love is dead, didn't Max tell you that?'

'Yes, but the accident was two years ago, and two years is a long time.'

Guileless and trusting as a child, Evelyn thought, and like a child expecting all her friends to love each other. It did not seem to occur to her that if Evelyn did love Max she might try to detach him from herself, and a less scrupulous girl might.

Sophy moved away to the window, and with her face raised towards the light, said apparently inconsequently:

'I am very fond of books and poetry, and you have a lovely voice.'

Puzzled, Evelyn stared at her. 'Thank you,' she said inadequately.

'Poetry should be read aloud. You would read it well.'

'I'm not an actress, Sophy.'

Sophy turned towards her. 'What I want to say is difficult, Eva, I fear to give offence. Anneliese, you know,

149

is leaving me, and in any case after the operation I shall be for a long time in a nursing home. It is a private one – Papa is very good, he does everything for my comfort. I read books in Braille, German ones, but there are many English ones I would like to meet ... to have read to me while I am convalescing.' She moved across the room so swiftly that Evelyn feared she might slip. Sophy dropped on her knees beside her, gripping her hands.

'You could help me so much,' she was almost pleading. 'You are kind and sympathetic. You could read to me during my long, solitary hours, and if ... if I can see, I shall have to learn to read and write all over again. I want you to be my ... my companion, Eva. Max said that he thought you might be wanting some ... some occupation.'

'Oh, did he!' Evelyn exclaimed in exasperation. Really, Max was far too officious! Yet when she had mentioned only that morning that she would have to find work, he had not appeared interested. He must have rushed off to see Sophy and between them they had concocted this position for her, companion help to Sophy. Did he really think she could accept such a situation?

'Papa will find you accommodation in Wien,' Sophy said diffidently, 'and of course ... this is difficult ... he will give you plenty of money.'

Vienna and Max, no parting of the ways. But Max coming round daily to visit Sophy, their marriage drawing nearer every hour. She could not bear that.

'I'm awfully sorry, Sophy,' she said gently, 'but really I couldn't. It would be most unsuitable.'

Sophy sighed and said no more. Evelyn hoped the subject was closed, but she had yet to reckon with Herr Hartmann, and lastly, Max.

He returned from his band contest in excellent spirits,

by which time Evelyn had been regaled with an enormous tea and endured an embarrassing interview with Herr Hartmann. He had, in his peculiar English, indicated with the utmost delicacy that he understood she needed a well-paid job, and since his daughter had taken such a great fancy to her, he was willing to gratify Sophy and pay her handsomely for her services.

Evelyn expressed herself honoured, but explained that her parents were expecting her to return to England.

Max was more forthright. He cornered her in the garden, screened from the house by weeping willows.

'You cannot afford to turn this very opportune offer down, Eve. You are untrained for anything, except teaching the pianoforte, which is poorly paid. Nobody else will give you what Herr Hartmann is willing to give you. Your parents, I imagine, will be greatly relieved to discover you are capable of supporting yourself.'

He need not have said that, Evelyn thought, wincing. She knew they would be delighted, not so much from the financial angle, but because she would be making a new life for herself. But if he could be plain-spoken, so could she.

'I don't want charity jobs found for me,' she said coldly, 'and after ... after what happened on the way back from Munich, you must realize I'm quite the wrong person to look after Sophy.'

'This isn't charity. Sophy will have to have some sort of companion since Anneliese is going, and as regards Munich, you yourself declared that that regrettable incident is closed. As far as I am concerned, it is consigned to oblivion, we were both rather overwrought and forgot ourselves.'

That stung her. 'I'm not surprised you want to forget it,' she said acidly.

He smiled sardonically. 'Do you mean that you wish to perpetuate it?' he asked, but his watching eyes had become eager.

'Of course not,' she said quickly.

'*Ach so*, but we must not let such trivial matters interfere with what is important.'

Trivial! So that was how he really regarded the interlude.

'Vienna is a pleasant city,' he went on, 'Sophy will not be exacting. What is your real reason for refusing?'

'I have explained all that,' she told him, averting her eyes.

'No, you have not.' He came closer to her, putting his hands on her shoulders, forcing her to look at him. 'Is it on my account that you do not wish to come? You have decided that I am not to be trusted?'

That was very nearly the truth. Summoning all her resolution, Evelyn tried to meet the close scrutiny of his very blue eyes, but hers wavered, and she dropped her lashes.

'You flatter yourself,' she said a little scornfully. 'Of course I don't think that.'

'I believe you do, but set your heart at rest. I shall be concerned only with Sophy. Could you not think of her also? This operation may not be successful, and we have all built such hopes upon it, and whether it is or not, it will be an ordeal for her. There is not a lot we can do to help her, or much that we can give her. She wants you.'

Evelyn twisted free from his grip upon her shoulders, and turned her back to him. Before her eyes the greens and golds of the garden shimmered through the moisture which had risen to her eyes.

'Oh, Max!' she whispered desperately.

Was the man quite blind? Could he not realize that to

act as Sophy's friend and confidant would be nearly as big an ordeal for her as the one the Austrian girl was facing?

'Well, what?' Curt and sharp. He was losing patience with her.

Naturally he did not know what she was feeling. She had deliberately misled him, pretending Harry was still the only man in her life, because she did not want him to suspect the true state of her heart. So it was hardly fair to blame him for misunderstanding her. Bracing herself, she turned back to face him.

'Nothing,' she said flatly.

'Eve, please do this for Sophy's sake,' he besought her, earnestly.

She did not reply, and seeing the lack of response in her face, he added coldly:

'Is it impossible for you to think of anyone but yourself?'

'You're calling me selfish?' she flashed.

'You have not given me any reason to think otherwise,' he retorted. 'But perhaps selfish is too harsh a word. Egotistical would be more correct.'

Which meant the same thing, but it was an unjust accusation. When he had first met her, she had been an egoist, completely wrapped up in her grief and despair, but she had been trying so hard to come out of her self-absorption, to mingle with other people, and she had resisted the temptation to try to detach him from Sophy. Even this visit to the Harmanns was not of her choosing, and her reason for refusing Sophy's request was because for all their sakes, she did not think that she ought to risk further contact with Max.

She wanted very much to go to Vienna, to see his home town and to postpone the inevitable parting from him.

But the very keenness of her desire warned her that it would be most unwise to yield to it.

Though he was choosing to ignore it, there was indubitably a strong physical attraction between Max and herself. She was feeling it at that moment. At any second some unforeseen incident might cause it to flare up, as it had on the Karer, and coming back from Munich. It was like sitting on a keg of gunpowder. Perhaps he would not mind if it did erupt, but that would only hurt her more, and be unfair to Sophy. She really had no option but to continue to refuse, and it was hard that what was in reality an unselfish act should be dubbed egotism.

Wishing to bring the present uncomfortable interview to an end, she said non-committally:

'Very well, I'll think about it.'

'There is not much time for thinking,' he urged, 'she goes next week.'

And so do you, she thought with a swift dart of pain. Could she withstand further persuasion when she wanted so much to go? Just to be in the same town as he was would be something. It looked as if she would have to recourse to flight.

Max must have told Amy about the proposal, before he encountered her, possibly hoping that she would be an ally, but here he had miscalculated, for Amy was dead against it.

Upon their return to the house, she expressed her objections at some length. Evelyn was far too young and unsophisticated to live unchaperoned in a wicked city like Vienna 'Is it wicked?' Evelyn queried. 'I don't suppose it is any worse than London.' She had never really lived on her own, she had always had a protector.

Evelyn became annoyed. Amy seemed to think that she had never been out of leading strings. She assured her that she was perfectly capable of looking after herself.

Amy became more outspoken. Fortunately the Hartmanns had left them alone to discuss the matter. Max seemed to be instigating the arrangement. Foreigners had such peculiar ideas regarding women, and Evelyn was such an innocent. Evelyn's cheeks flamed:

'You're insulting us both! Max thinks only of Sophy, and I wouldn't dream of coming between them,' forgetting in her indignation that she had similar doubts herself.

Perversely it was Amy's opposition which drove her into acceptance, for when Max appeared with Herr Hartmann and Amy began to say that her niece could not possibly consider such a proposition, Eve contradicted her flatly and told the two men that she was prepared to go to Vienna as soon as Sophy was installed there.

Tactfully Max smoothed down the ruffled Amy, telling her that the Hartmanns would be there for the first crucial days and they would take good care of Evelyn.

As she walked with him to his car in advance of Amy, trying to excuse her aunt, for Amy had been almost rude, his expressions of relief and gratitude seemed far in excess of what the circumstances required. She was fairly certain that Sophy had only suggested the job to him that same day, upon hearing about Evelyn's circumstances. Sophy's sudden desire for her company, even if Anneliese were leaving, was a little surprising.

Uneasily she began to wonder if Amy were right, and some sinister motive lay behind the proposed arrangement, but it was too late to draw back. By devious means, Max had again managed to direct her fate, and she must abide by the consequences.

CHAPTER EIGHT

HERR HARTMANN procured for Evelyn a small two-roomed flat not far from the private hospital where Sophy was installed. He and his wife were staying at a hotel, but as the English girl's visit would be of much longer duration than theirs, he thought the flat would be more convenient for her. Evelyn agreed; she much preferred being on her own.

Sophy was in a private ward, and she had to undergo various preparatory treatments. Evelyn was allowed to visit her at stated times, and these did not coincide with Max's visits. He seemed to be avoiding her, and she realized that her suspicions of an ulterior motive for his persuasions were quite unfounded.

She found Sophy was apprehensive and nervous, not so much fearing the operation but what its success implied. The new world she was about to enter would effect such an enormous change in her life. It soothed her to have Evelyn read poetry to her; she had been quite sincere when she had said she enjoyed it. She did not care for modern works, liking rhyme and rhythm: the sonorous roll of Shakespeare and Milton appealed to her. Language, Evelyn discovered, had its own music. Sophy told her that she must learn German so that she could enjoy Goethe.

Herr Hartmann wanted to know everything about their sessions together, when Evelyn dined with the anxious parents, which she did every night.

Once when he was alone with her, he said a little sadly:

'If it has the success, I fear we lose our Sophy.'

'Surely not!' Evelyn exclaimed, and quoted the old tag about a daughter being a daughter all her life.

'*Ach so*, we see her often, no doubt, but it is not the same.'

Evelyn was about to mention grandchildren, but was a little shy of doing so. Herr Hartmann might think she was being a little too familiar, but he would in all probability have that joy to come. Max and Sophy should have lovely children, Evelyn thought wistfully, but found it difficult to visualize Sophy as a mother. In some ways she still seemed to be a child herself.

Evelyn spent her free time exploring the city and went on an expedition out to the Vienna woods. Here there were hills, but she missed the mountains. She could understand why Max loved the Tyrol. She thought of him a great deal and wondered where he lived with his mother and whether if she had the opportunity she dared ask him about it.

She saw the Hofburg, that great pile of buildings which had been the residence of the Hapsburg monarchs, and reflected upon the tragic life of the last of them, Franz Josef, whose adored wife had been mortally wounded by an assassin, whose son had shot himself with his mistress at Mayerling and whose nephew and heir had been killed at Sarajevo, thereby initiating a war which had lost the Empire a large portion of its territories.

Such epic tragedies made her own losses seem insignificant.

Then followed a day of acute anxiety while the operation was being performed. Evelyn spent it with the Hartmanns, and for the first time since coming to Vienna, she saw Max. He came to support Sophy's parents during their hours of suspense. They had been persuaded not to wait at the hospital, for it would be a long business, but they could not bear to leave the hotel in case the telephone rang.

When Max came into the room, Evelyn's heart seemed to turn over and she could not meet his eyes. Mutely she extended her hand, and he took it in a firm clasp, his regard a question, but his words were formal:

'*Grüss Gott*, Eve, you are looking well, so I trust you are not finding your duties too onerous?'

'Not in the least, and I'm glad to be able to do something for Sophy.'

'Eve has given our daughter much solace,' Frau Hartmann informed him. 'I do not know what she would have done without her. But do you not at the hospital meet?'

Max released Evelyn's hand and smiled sardonically.

'By ill luck our visits never seem to coincide.'

Ill luck! She knew very well that he made his plans so that they should not coincide.

He turned from her to talk to the Hartmanns, and being more or less ignored, Evelyn was able to study him without being observed.

She saw that he was thinner, always lean; there seemed to be no spare flesh upon him at all. The suit he was wearing, once a perfect fit, hung slackly from his shoulders, and there were dark smudges under his eyes. The long wait to learn Sophy's fate – and his – was evidently telling upon him.

A chance remark of Herr Hartmann's roused her to a new alarm. She had not understood before that the operation could be actually dangerous, the eyes being connected with the brain.

Max was saying: 'If she does not recover from it, I shall never forgive myself, for it was I who persuaded her to have it done.'

'*Nein, nein,*' Herr Hartmann protested, laying his hand upon the younger man's shoulder. 'We all wished for it to be done. You cannot sole responsibility assume,' and he relapsed into German.

Max smiled but looked unconvinced. He knew that Sophy would have yielded to no persuasion except his.

Evelyn's heart went out to him in a surge of love and sympathy, while she prayed wordlessly that Sophy would come through successfully.

Seeing Max again, she knew that her own love for him was even stronger and deeper than before, but she wanted his happiness above her own – his and Sophy's, but she was afraid.

Life, she thought, could be so cruelly ironic. She, who would have gladly died after her accident, had survived, and it would be too dreadful if Sophy, who had so much to live for, did not. That she might benefit if Sophy died never once crossed her mind, for her new love contained little or nothing of self.

They made a pretence of eating lunch. Max's face was drawn with anxiety, but when they were back in the Hartmanns' suite, he did his best to distract the distraught parents. They talked about the opera, the productions which were to be selected for the next season. Max wanted to import one by a well-known modern British composer, and appealed to Evelyn for her opinion of his work. That led to a discussion upon modern music as opposed to the classics. Max did not admire the more avant-garde; it was, he said, like a mathematical exercise. The test of any work was the pleasure it gave to the listener, and that led to an argument as to whether on that premise, the popular songs of the day were not the greatest music; upon which subject they all became so animated, they almost forgot why they were there.

The shrilling of the telephone brought them back to reality with a sense of shock. Herr Hartmann snatched off the receiver. They watched tensely until he replaced it, wiping his brow.

'It has been done,' he said, 'and all is well. She is still under the anaesthetic, but we may see her tomorrow.'

Max jumped to his feet, relief erasing the lines from his face.

'Come along, Eve,' he ordered. 'Let us go out and get some fresh air. I must order some flowers to be sent to her.' He had been sending every day. 'She can smell them even if she cannot see them.'

'But God willing, she will,' Frau Hartmann said piously.

They would not know until the dressings were taken off whether the operation had been successful.

The sunlit streets were a relief after the oppressive atmosphere of the suite during their long visit. The florist was stocked with the blossoms of late spring, irises, late tulips, early roses, carnations, lilies, snowy heads of white lilac and more exotic orchids.

Max chose the flowers for their scent, lilies and roses. While the assistant took down the address to which they were to be sent, he spied a bowl of dark red damask rose buds made up into posies, and indicated them, speaking in German. The girl took one out, wiping the stems, and handed it to Max. He passed it to Evelyn.

'For me?' she exclaimed, gratified.

'For you. They are your colour.'

She was wearing a black crimplene suit from her old wardrobe, but she had lightened its sombreness with a yellow blouse. The assistant produced a large pin and fastened the roses on to the lapel of her jacket. That done, they went back into the street.

'The first time I saw you, you were wearing a crimson dress,' Max remarked.

'Fancy remembering after all this time!'

'It made a very strong impression. You, in your red gown, your pale face and night-dark hair and the sounds which you produced from that great instrument ... I do not know which were more ravished, my eyes or my ears.'

'Please don't,' she said, for the memory was poignant.

He drew her arm through his. 'Can you not look back without pain?' he asked. 'That was an experience which we shared.'

'Like Munich?' she asked, withdrawing her arm. 'I don't think you should be reminding me of such occasions while Sophy is so ill.'

'But she is going to be all right,' he insisted. 'There is no need to wear mourning faces for her now. We can rejoice.'

'It depends how,' she said significantly.

They walked a few paces in silence, and then he asked in a different tone:

'What would you like to do now?'

'I would like to see your home,' she said impulsively.

'And I would like to show it to you, but it is some way out. We will take a taxi.'

The house stood alone in a shaded garden, with glimpses of the river Danube – alas, not blue but brown – in the distance. It was low and rambling with flower-filled window boxes before the latticed windows. Inside, the wainscoted rooms were low-ceilinged with exposed oak beams, which made it a little dark, but it had a friendly, homely atmosphere.

He took her into the music room – of course there

would be a music room – with french windows wide open to the lawn, and a polished wood floor. There were books in shelves filling one wall, a low wooden couch with a crimson throw-over, and a great gilded harp in one corner. Busts of Beethoven and Mozart stood on the mantelpiece, above which was a Degas painting of ballet dancers. There was a grand piano, a Bechstein, and Evelyn's eyes went to it at once.

'Do you play it?'

'Sometimes.' He raised the lid from the keyboard and ran his fingers over the notes. He had a musician's touch. Raising his head, he met her wistful eyes.

'Come, you play the treble and I will play the bass.'

He struck soft chords from a Mozart study which she knew well. Her right hand went almost without conscious volition to the keys, picking out the tune. Softly, with his left, he filled in the bass. His right hand closed round her left, hanging by her side.

'We could play a duet.' There was subtle meaning in his low voice; a duet meant a pair, two together. Their shoulders touched as they stood before the instrument which they both loved. The melody increased in volume, echoing round the pleasant room. They were in perfect harmony, perfect accord. It was more than a touching of bodies, it had become a communion of spirits.

Then Evelyn struck a wrong note. She pulled her hand from his and turned away with a choking sensation.

'I . . . I think I ought to go.'

'Why so suddenly? I thought you would like a cup of tea. My mother is resting, but I will call her.'

He moved towards the door.

'No, please, don't disturb her. Really I must go.'

She should not be here, this was to be Sophy's home and in it there was no place for her. That moment of close intimacy with Max had unnerved her. If she stayed, God alone knew what folly she might commit – some desperate plea for recognition, for inclusion in his life upon any terms. And Sophy trusted her, Sophy who was lying in hospital upheld by her faith in her lover.

'You will not disturb her,' Max told her. 'Her siesta time is over, and I think I hear her moving upstairs.'

'There . . . there may be more news of Sophy.'

'I do not expect there will be any more this afternoon. I shall call round last thing, of course.' He was looking at her questioningly. 'I would like you to meet my mother.'

'Some other time, but . . . but I'd like to go back now. I'm rather tired.'

When she wanted desperately to stay, wanted Max to take her in his arms. Every moment she remained in that sunlit room made it harder to go. The friendly atmosphere, the piano, Max himself, with a light in his eyes which she could not interpret – it was not the kindling of passion, and certainly not polite regret – were calling to her to stay, but she dared no longer share their intimacy.

Max took a step towards her.

'Evelyn,' he said. His voice was low and pleading.

Hastily she drew back and his face hardened while the light left his eyes.

'If you are tired that is another matter. I will put you in a taxi and you can return to your flat.' He spoke coldly.

'Thank you,' she murmured, and passed before him out of the room.

Then followed days of suspense, days while Sophy lay with her head held immobile between sandbags, patiently waiting while her wounds healed, and Evelyn tried to distract her with poetry and prose. There was a radio in the room, but she said she infinitely preferred to hear Evelyn's voice, and they could select their programme and not merely accept what was offered to them.

'I can listen to that when I am alone,' Sophy pointed out. 'I like a change when you are here.'

And that was what Evelyn was being paid to provide.

The Hartmanns returned to Innsbruck, and Sophy was dependent upon her and Max for her visitors, and of course her confessor. About that side of her life, Sophy never spoke to Evelyn, who realized with wry amusement that she was considered a heretic.

Max never appeared during the hours she spent with Sophy, but occasionally she met him either coming in or going out. He greeted her distantly, as if she were a stranger. His chill politeness hurt, but she had sense enough to know she could expect no more.

Sophy's twenty-first birthday occurred while she was in hospital. Evelyn had sent to England to obtain for her a volume of Swinburne, thinking that she would like that poet's rich cadences. When Evelyn came in on that morning, she found the room decked with fresh flowers and various gifts were strewn on the bed. The sandbags, to Sophy's relief, had been removed.

Sophy fingered the book lovingly, when Evelyn had presented it with her good wishes.

'Soon perhaps I shall see it.' She lay back on her pillows. 'Eva, I have much worry about Max. He is so low-spirited, though he try to hide it. I think he is most unhappy.'

'He must be very worried about you,' Evelyn pointed out.

'*Ach*, no, it is not that. I grow more strong every day,

164

and if the operation is a failure I shall be no worse than I was before.'

'But isn't it ... very important to him ... that it should succeed?' Evelyn asked, stumbling over her words, for did not Sophy's marriage hang upon the recovery of her sight?

'It will make no difference to him,' Sophy said confidently. 'He is used to me as I was.'

She reached towards her bedside table and Evelyn hastened to assist her.

'What is it you want?'

'There should be a small packet on there. I wish that you look at it, Eva.'

It was a small box. Evelyn opened it and looked at the ring which it contained. So Sophy had decided to marry Max with or without her vision.

'Is it not pretty?' Sophy asked. The ring bore a small ruby heart, surrounded with tiny brilliants. 'Max said it was. It is in the shape of a heart, *nicht wahr*? Once when I was very small girl, I said I wanted a ring like a heart, and Max said he would give me one when I was twenty-one. Of course I did not know for what I asked, but Max remembered. He said it was his heart, and it will be the first thing I shall see when I open my eyes, because, even if I can only see dimly, it will sparkle. Does it sparkle?'

'Yes,' Evelyn assured her, moving it to and fro to catch the light. 'That was a very pretty thought of Max's.'

'He is like that,' Sophy said happily.

'Won't you put it on?' Evelyn asked hardily, stifling her pain. 'He will like to see you wearing it.'

'Should I?' Sophy stretched out her right hand. About to say 'the other one', Evelyn checked; had she not been told that continentals wore their engagement rings on their right hands? Sophy knew better than she did. She slipped it on to the third finger, and Sophy gave a sigh of satisfaction.

'I love Max,' she said simply. 'I love you too, Eva.'

'You're a dear thing,' Evelyn told her warmly. Any jealousy she had felt of Sophy had long since died. Nobody could be jealous of such a child. Max, she thought, would have to make a woman of her. But the sight of the ring had given her a pang.

Came the morning when, entering Sophy's room, Evelyn found it shadowed by drawn curtains and Sophy a dim figure against her pillows, wearing dark glasses instead of bandages.

'Oh, Eva, Eva,' she cried exultantly, 'I have seen the light!'

Little by little she was allowed to use her newly acquired vision. Soon she would be going home and Evelyn was to go with her to stay indefinitely in Innsbruck.

The first time Sophy saw Evelyn's face – through the dark glasses – she stared at her for a long time, then drawing a deep breath, she said:

'I am not disappointed. You are just as I imagined you would be.'

'I hope I shall never disappoint you in any way,' Evelyn told her. She meant it. Resolutely she put all thought of Max away from her. She would be leaving Vienna, but she had seen little of him during her stay there. He would not be able to come often to Innsbruck, and she was glad of that. His presence still disturbed her, and she wanted to be completely loyal to Sophy, but her resolution was to be severely tested before she left.

On Sophy's last day at the hospital, Evelyn was reading to her from the 'Atalanta in Calydon'.

'Sweet days befall them and good loves and lords,
And tender temperate honours of the hearth,
Peace and a perfect life and blameless bed.'

She was thinking that Althaea's wish for the two unhappy sisters, Clytemnestra and Helen, was a fair picture
of what Sophy's married life would be, especially the
tender, temperate honours of the hearth, when Max
walked in. Astonished to see him, Evelyn laid down the
book and rose to take her leave.

'You must not go yet,' Sophy commanded. 'Max is
going to take you out to dinner and the opera. He is not
engaged tonight, and we planned it yesterday. You deserve a treat after bearing with me for so long.'

'I've no dress,' Evelyn said quickly, jumping at the first
excuse that presented itself.

'No?' Max queried. 'What has become of the apricot
creation which you wore at Munich? That would be very
suitable.'

It was hanging in her wardrobe at her flat. Max, she
saw, was looking arrogantly sure of himself. She glanced
despairingly at Sophy. Was the girl really so obtuse?

Apparently so, for she continued to insist that Evelyn
must go. The opera was 'Carmen', and she had heard her
say that Bizet's music always excited her, so when Max
had mentioned it, she had thought of Evelyn at once.
Evelyn saw that it would be impossible to disappoint her
and that she must appear to acquiesce.

Max blandly made arrangements to meet her outside
her flat that evening, and she again tried to take her leave.

'I have the car outside, I will run you back,' he said.

'But aren't you going to stay with Sophy?'

'He will drop in tomorrow to say good-bye before we
leave,' Sophy told her. 'Now I ought to rest. You will tell
me all about the opera, will you not, Max, and how Eva

looked in the apricot dress?'

'To be sure I will,' Max promised, and stooped to kiss her.

Outside, Evelyn turned upon him. 'Of course I'm not coming.'

'Of course you are. What will Sophy say to you if you do not?'

'She needn't know.'

'She will know. If you can invent an account of a fictitious evening together, I cannot. What are you afraid of, Eve? Do you imagine I am intending to rape you in a box at my own opera house?'

Evelyn's cheeks flamed. 'Don't be so absurd!'

'It is you who are absurd. You will be ready to come with me tonight, and you will wear your golden dress. It is very fitting that we should end our association with music.'

The words struck like a knell at her heart. This might well be the last time she would ever be alone with him, might even be the last time she saw him, for she did not know how long she would be staying with the Hartmanns. She would like to leave before the preparations for Sophy's wedding began.

'You can't really want to spend a whole evening with me,' she said doubtfully.

'Now whatever makes you say that? So far the times we have spent together have been highly diverting from my point of view, and I do not think you have found my company dull.'

'You'll get no diversion tonight,' she flashed at him.

'No, I am afraid there will be no opportunity, as we shall be in public places.' He dropped his mocking manner, and went on sincerely, '*Ach,* Eve, do not treat me like the big, bad wolf in the fairy story. I agree with

Sophy, you deserve some fun, and she has given us her blessing.'

Finally she agreed to go. Max always bested her scruples in the end, she thought, as she took out her evening dress. He liked to have his own way, and since both he and his fiancée were so insistent upon this outing, she could not be blamed if it had an unplanned sequel. But there was no reason why that should occur. She believed that Max quite genuinely wished to give her an evening's pleasure, prompted by Sophy of course. Unfortunately 'Carmen' always stirred her blood, made her feel elemental. She would simply have to make herself behave like a civilized young lady, that was all.

All went well. In the restaurant with its shaded lights, its rococo decor suggesting the elegancies of a former period, Max played the perfect host.

He gave her Hungarian Tokay to drink, and warned her that it was potent. Avoiding personal matters, they talked about music. He told her she must visit Salzburg before she left the country. Mozart still reigned there. There were memorials to his memory all over the place and a museum devoted to his relics.

The opera was one long enchantment. Evelyn was still young enough to like to see her music dressed up. There was a superb Carmen, a vivid burning creature, who had not yet put on weight.

'I always shrink from engaging heavyweights,' Max told her in the interval, 'but sometimes it is inevitable, especially for Wagner, and the voice is what is important. Opera is a completely unrealistic art form. We are asked to accept that in moments of emotion it is natural for people to express their deepest feelings in top Cs or basso profundo at inordinate length.'

'I could express mine that way,' Evelyn said, thinking

169

of her piano.

'I have known you to use more satisfying methods,' and he gave her a mischievous look.

'None of that, please,' Evelyn admonished him, as the curtain rose on a flamboyant Spanish scene. Throughout the evening there had been an undercurrent, sly references to her former indiscretions, but since he had given Sophy a ring, he could not be such a heel as to be contemplating making any further advances.

Carmen died, and Don José made his piteous confession, the curtain fell.

'He spoilt it all,' Max commented as they left the theatre. 'If a man ruins himself for a woman and she plays him false, kill her by all means, but do not regret it.'

'He still loved her,' Evelyn reminded him. 'Sometimes you sound awfully hard, Max.'

'Would you appreciate a soft man?' he asked jeeringly, as he helped her into his car, and started the engine. 'It is a beautiful night and I am sure you are too excited to sleep. Shall we drive around for a while?'

She ought to say no, but the music was still surging through her veins, it *was* a beautiful night, and she knew that she would not sleep. Moreover, on the morrow she would have to say good-bye to Max.

'That would be nice,' she said.

He drove out of the town into the moonwashed countryside, and she sat beside him lost in her dreams, in which Max and the Toreador were mingled.

On the edge of a wooded grove he came to a halt.

'Are you sure you are not making a mistake?' he asked harshly.

Eve came out of dreamland with a start. 'What do you mean?'

'What I say. In persisting in clinging to a sentimental memory, you are throwing away the substance for the shadow. You are not indifferent to me, that I have ascertained. Why must you continue to deny yourself ... and me?'

'Oh, you're outrageous!' she cried. 'How can you make such suggestions, when you're engaged to Sophy? You're insulting me and you'll break her heart.'

'Sophy?' he asked blankly. 'Sophy?'

'She loves and trusts you, you know that. She wears your ring.'

'*Ach*, that! That was just a redeeming of a childhood's promise.' She saw he was looking at her with troubled eyes. 'You do not mean that she is in love with me?'

'Didn't you know it?' Evelyn asked incredulously. 'That was why she underwent the operation, so she could become your wife – and surely you love her?'

'I adore her, I admire her, but that is not being in love. Eve, you have shocked me. I never dreamed of it.'

'Then you were blind!'

'So was she,' he observed dryly. 'Otherwise she would have seen ... poor child, she lives in a world of fantasy.'

'But you can't let her down.'

'No, I cannot, can I? If this is true.'

'It sticks out a mile, Max, in everything she does and says, but she hesitated to marry you while she was blind. She told me when I visited her on that first day that only by gaining her sight could she win her heart's desire.'

'And you are convinced she meant myself?'

'There is no one else, is there?'

'Not that I know of. But little Sophy! I have always thought of her as a delightful child.'

'Children grow up,' Evelyn remarked dryly. 'Hadn't you noticed that she had?'

Loyalty and genuine affection were prompting her to plead Sophy's cause, but she wondered how Max could have been so dim. He must have realized that he was arousing expectations in the girl. He had even given her a ring.

'On the Karer Pass you talked of cherishing and serving the girl you hoped to marry,' Evelyn went on. 'When I met Sophy and saw you with her, I believed she was that girl. And if I thought so, how much more reason had she for doing so?'

She looked at him accusingly. Mention of the Karer brought his attention back to her.

'If you believed that you must have also believed I was an outsize in cads to act as I did towards you.'

'It didn't enhance my opinion of you,' she said honestly.

'Which never has been very good,' he remarked dryly, 'but I am beginning to see daylight.' He was silent, apparently digesting her revelation. Then he sighed, and asked:

'You consider it is my duty to marry Sophy?'

For a second she hesitated. In the past few moments she had learned that Max was not in love with Sophy. He might even have some regard for herself – then remembering Sophy's innocent trust in this man, she said firmly:

'I know honour isn't a fashionable word nowadays, but if you have a spark of it, you must marry Sophy. You wouldn't want to break her heart, would you?'

'God forbid that I should ever cause her to suffer,' he said fervently. 'But I am not convinced that you are right. However, you seem to have no doubt about it.'

'Nor will you when you've thought about it.'

'I am doing that now, and the situation presents more

possibilities than one.' His voice became sardonic. 'You are an expert at sacrifices, are you not? Are you presenting yourself as a burnt offering to Sophy now?'

'I don't know what you mean,' she retorted, though she had an inkling, but she resented his sarcastic tone. She was ready to disregard her own interests to obtain Sophy's happiness, but she expected Max to admire and praise her unselfishness, instead of which he referred to it as a burnt offering.

'You do, but your pride will not let you admit it,' he told her savagely. He pressed the starter. 'I give up! I have tried to teach you how to live again, but you prefer to bury yourself in self-immolation and insult me for my pains. Sophy will be my only concern in future.'

'That is as it should be,' she said, trying to keep her lips from trembling.

'And that is your last word?'

'There's nothing more to say.'

He sent the car hurtling back to the town and he did not speak again beyond a curt good night when he dropped her at her door.

Evelyn crept up to her bed and wept as if her heart would break.

CHAPTER NINE

Sophy's recovery was considered a great achievement by medical science and brought her some very unwelcome publicity. She left the hospital through a barrage of snapping cameras and upon her return home was plagued by reporters and requests for interviews. Eventually the nine days' wonder was superseded by something more sensational and she was left in peace.

Her vision improved every day and her first week at home was a voyage of discovery as she exclaimed in wonder at the appearance of each familiar object. Some she was frankly disgusted with, others exceeded her expectations. The mountains, she said, were exactly as she had imagined them.

As Sophy became daily more independent and even began to read to herself, Evelyn began to think about returning to England. She felt she was imposing upon the Hartmanns' generosity.

Amy had left Seefeld soon after Evelyn had gone to Vienna. Though she had disapproved of her niece's course of action, she did not bear malice, and wrote saying she hoped to see her soon, since Sophy had so miraculously recovered, which Evelyn construed as a broad hint that it was time she left.

During the first few weeks, Max did not put in an appearance, though he rang Sophy nearly every day. Once on passing through the hall while Sophy was at the instrument, the girl called to her:

'Would you not like to speak to Max?'

A crackle from the instrument indicated some protest.

Sophy replied in German and Evelyn made her escape.

Afterwards, she saw Sophy looking at her with a worried expression, but she said nothing. She must be wondering why she and Max had apparently quarrelled, but Evelyn could not enlighten her.

As the days passed, Sophy seemed to become more and more withdrawn, and Evelyn became indignant with Max. The girl was obviously pining for her lover and he was treating her shabbily by not coming to see her. Surely, however busy he was, he could find time for a flying visit? Possibly he wanted to avoid meeting herself, and that idea made her hasten her arrangements for departure.

That the Hartmanns were anxious about their daughter was apparent in the way they watched her. They spoke of Max from time to time, but nothing was said of wedding preparations. There was a certain tension in the atmosphere as if they were all waiting for some crisis to occur. Evelyn wondered if Max were stalling, but she hardly thought he would do that, since he had declared he would make Sophy his first concern.

Because she sensed the ground was delicate, she made no inquiries about Sophy's plans, but pressed on with her own.

Rather to her chagrin, Sophy seemed perfectly reconciled to losing her, until she said:

'It is well you make some provision for your future, Eva, because I shall be leaving Innsbruck soon.'

In her relief at this intelligence, Evelyn exclaimed involuntarily:

'So Max has come up to scratch!'

'What strange things you say – Max does not scratch,' and Sophy giggled. 'We arranged over the telephone that he is to fetch me next Sunday to see what I hope will be my new home. I am to spend the night with his mother to rest before the journey back. Before long I hope that I go there for good.'

Evelyn turned away so that Sophy could not see her face, while before her eyes swam a vision of that long, low room, the Bechstein piano, before which she had stood with Max – what might have been.

'Have you ... have you fixed the date?' she asked, thinking that Sophy was being a little secretive about her wedding.

'That has yet to be decided,' Sophy told her. 'It does not depend upon me alone, you understand.'

'Of course not.'

She hoped that it would not occur to Sophy to ask her to be her bridesmaid, there were limits to her endurance, but the fact that she belonged to a different denomination would probably preclude that, she remembered with relief. As soon as the wedding date was fixed, she would take her leave.

'I hope you will be very happy,' she said mechanically.

Sophy's face was ecstatic.

'It will be the fulfilment of my dearest hopes.'

She glanced at Evelyn's unresponsive back, and asked diffidently:

'When Max comes to fetch me, you will be nice to him, will you not? He has not seen you for a long time.'

'No longer than since he has seen you,' Evelyn pointed out, 'and he won't have time to talk to me, you'll be in a hurry to get away.'

She intended to avoid seeing Max if she could.

Sophy's delicate brows puckered.

'But I thought that you had an affection for him. Is it that you have quarrelled? He did not want to speak to you on the telephone. He does not talk about you any more.'

'Why should he?' Evelyn asked brusquely, thinking that in the circumstances she was hardly a suitable subject for discussion between Max and his fiancée.

'I do not like my friends to be estranged,' Sophy said naïvely. 'Can you not tell me what it is all about?'

Evelyn laughed. Sophy was the last person to whom she could confide what had occurred. 'Oh, we're quite good friends,' she told her, trying to speak casually, 'but I fancy he has other things on his mind just now. No doubt I'll be seeing him when you come back.'

For Max would be staying the night.

So Evelyn deliberately kept out of the way, when Max came to fetch Sophy. She heard his car arrive and the Hartmanns' welcoming voices. He refused to come in, saying he was pressed for time, and from the shelter of her bedroom balcony, Evelyn watched the departure.

Sophy's hand was on Max's arm and she was laughing gaily as he led her to the car. It reminded Evelyn of the first time she had seen them together. He helped her into the passenger seat, fastened her seat belt, and closed the door upon her as if she were something very precious.

Evelyn had a clear view of him as he walked round the car. So dear and so familiar, and completely inaccessible. He glanced up at the house, and she drew back hastily, hoping he had not seen her watching him. Then the car glided smoothly away.

They returned on the evening of the following day. When they heard the car, the Hartmanns went out into the hall to welcome them and Evelyn hovered uncertainly in the doorway of the sitting-room, half inclined to escape upstairs. Sophy's raptures about Max's home were going to be hard to bear.

Sophy came running in, her face radiant, and flung herself into her father's arms, babbling in German. Max followed. His eyes went to Evelyn and his expression was quizzical. Frau Hartmann was wiping away a tear.

Sophy extricated herself from her father, kissed her mother and came towards Evelyn.

'Eva, it is news most wonderful! I have seen the Reverend Mother. In six months' time I am to be accepted as a postulant!'

The room seemed to swirl round Evelyn. All she was conscious of, as Sophy kissed her, was Max's satirical grin.

They dined with the windows open to the mountains and the night. Sophy did not speak of her novitiate again. She had always been reserved about her religion, but she rattled on gaily about her journey, Max's house and Max's mother, both of which she declared had come up to her expectations now she could see them properly.

Her father said: 'You have always been the box that chatters, *liebling*. How, I wonder, will you endure the silence of the cloister?'

Evelyn understood now his grief at parting with her. The severance would be much greater than if Sophy had married. Sophy herself was superbly confident.

'That is why I talk so much now. Later I must learn to be more quiet.'

Evelyn waited with some trepidation throughout the meal for a sign from Max. Since now there was no barrier between them, surely he would come to her? A slight misgiving assailed her. He must have known for some time that she had been wrong about Sophy, but he had continued to avoid her. Perhaps he was punishing her for her doubts of him, and for misleading him about the girl's feelings. He never glanced her way, nor did he address her directly, but seemed absorbed in Sophy's chatter.

She resolved that she must speak to him and clear up the misunderstanding, if misunderstanding there were. Tonight would be her last chance.

As bedtime drew near, he went out into the garden for a final smoke, and seizing her opportunity, she slipped out after him.

It was a clear, starlit night, the last light still faintly illuminating the western sky, the mountains humped against it. Max was a dark shape beside a weeping willow, identifiable by the red tip of his cigar. In her pale dress – it was the grey one in which she had danced with him, brightened by her green stole – Evelyn was like a ghost gliding across the shadowed garden.

'Max?' she called, as she approached him.

'At your service.' His tone was cold. He threw down his cigar butt, it fell in a shower of sparks and he set his foot upon it. She waited, but he said nothing. Finally in desperation, she stammered:

'I . . . I've come to apologize. It was a perfectly genuine misunderstanding.'

He folded his arms. She could not see his face, but he seemed to be looking at her, for she, in her light dress, was more visible than he was. His form was barely perceptible against the tree behind him.

'Was it?' Two words with a crack like a whip.

'Yes . . . and when I told you, you accepted the explanation. You believed it was true too.'

'Not altogether. I have always known Sophy was drawn to the religious life, but a young girl's emotional reactions are not very reliable. Your deductions surprised me, but they were possibly true. Sophy's recovery might have turned her mind in a more worldly direction and my conscience smote me. I feared that she had mistaken my fraternal affection for something quite different. However, she soon set my mind at rest, and before I had made a fool of myself by making a declaration. No thanks to you, though.'

The cold, embittered voice coming out of the dark, seemed like a disembodied accusation, she could hardly believe it was Max speaking, the man with whom she had hoped to be reconciled.

'I . . . I'm sorry,' she murmured inadequately, 'but you see . . .'

'No, I do not see,' he interrupted. 'You blow first hot, then cold, Eve, and that night you were arctic, but you could have found a more honest reason for repulsing me than dragging in poor Sophy.'

'I didn't . . .' she began, and stopped, while the conviction grew that nothing she could say would shake his misapprehension of her motives. Now she understood why he had not wanted to communicate with her when he had discovered her mistake, but it was an absurdly flimsy barrier if he had any feeling for her at all.

A little wind stirred the fronds of the weeping willow. Max took out his case and extricated another cigar. He flicked on his lighter and the flame illuminated his face. It was set and hard.

A new idea flashed into her mind. He *had* no feeling for her, and what was making him so bitter was Sophy's decision. Now she was unattainable, he had discovered that his love for her was not platonic at all, and he was venting his disappointment upon herself. To test her supposition, she said tentatively:

'Are you sorry that Sophy is going to become a nun?'

'Frankly, I am. Being a worldly creature myself, I feel it is rather a shame that all that prettiness and vivacity should be shut up in a convent when she could delight some man. A purely selfish and masculine point of view.' He laughed without mirth. 'But you know that I cannot appreciate the female urge to make sacrifices of themselves.'

'Burnt offerings was the term you used,' she returned. That phrase, 'when she could delight some man' struck at her heart. He was referring to himself.

'I believe it was, but in your case, you were not really sacrificing yourself, were you, Eve? Only me.'

'Max!'

'You always had an itch to dramatize yourself. When the Harry theme became threadbare, you offered yourself up for Sophy. Quite unnecessarily if you had taken the trouble to ascertain the facts. I, of course, was to be sacrificed too – quite a holocaust – but if you had cared a damn for me, you might have considered my feelings. Once I thought there was an affinity between us, I thought you still had a heart, but you were right when you said it died with Harry. What was between us had a not very pretty name, because all you can feel now is appetite.'

'Oh!' she cried distractedly. 'Oh, how can you!'

'I am being honest, which you were not, but I should not upbraid you for what you cannot help,' he said more gently. 'I hear that you are returning to England. Please give my regards to your estimable aunt when you see her again. Now you had better go in, or you will catch cold in that thin dress.'

It was dismissal, but she lingered, unable to accept that this was their final parting until he told her brutally:

'I am sorry, but I am in no mood to give you any diversion tonight, if that is what you are waiting for. I have had a surfeit of women and their devious ways. I feel inclined to follow Sophy's example and become a monk.

Good night, Eve.'

She ran from him then, devastated by the horrible things which he had said to her. 'All you can feel now is appetite.' The words seemed to scorch her brain. If that was how he interpreted her physical response to him, how he must despise her!

Sophy looked up eagerly when she re-entered the sitting-room, but her face fell when she saw that Evelyn was alone. Mechanically Evelyn said good night to the Hartmanns and crept away to bed.

Evelyn lay sleepless under her feather overlay, staring unseeingly into the dimness of the room. The french window on to the balcony was set wide open to the night. The black bulk of the Nordkette blocked the sky, but below it, a faint glow rose from the lights in the town, and late traffic was still passing beyond the garden. Then the lights began to go out, the traffic ceased and a brooding silence filled the valley.

She was revolving in her mind her tangled association with Max, and tangled indeed it had always been from their first meeting on the *alm* to the last dreadful scene tonight. Always he had vacillated between her and Sophy, his sacred and profane loves, she thought wryly, but to accuse her of deceiving him about the state of Sophy's affections was unfair. Anyone who had seen him with Sophy would have reached the same conclusions that she had done. Sophy had told her he seemed unhappy, and the reason was obvious; he had felt Sophy was slipping away from him and he could do nothing to keep her, having come to the full realization of his sentiments towards her too late. He had sought to salve the pride which Sophy had wounded, by accusing her of intentionally misleading him to effect a similar rejection, which he must know was untrue, but the breach between them was final now, there was no doubt about that.

Someone tapped softly upon her door, and Sophy pushed it open.

'Eva, are you asleep?'

'No, darling. Did you want anything?'

'Me? No. I have all that I ever wanted.' Sophy crossed the room and perched herself on the foot of Evelyn's bed. 'I wish everyone to be as happy as I am.'

'That's very sweet of you, but I'm afraid we can't all live on ecstatic peaks,' Evelyn told her. 'We have to have our ups and downs.'

'I know you have, but you are, how you say, rising up now, but it is Max for whom I am troubled. He is most miserable.'

'Perhaps it is because you are going into a convent,' Evelyn suggested.

'*Nein, nein*, that is not it. There has been nothing like that between me and Max, always he has been my big brother. No, Eva, it is you who make him unhappy.'

'Oh, Sophy, please,' Evelyn cried a little desperately, 'don't you try to add to the complications. Whoever Max is fretted about it's not I. He made that very plain to-night.'

'In some way you have hurt him,' Sophy said wisely, 'but he would never betray it. You see he loves you, he has loved you for a long time – it happened when he first saw you at that concert in London.'

'That's not very likely. People don't fall in love at first sight.'

'He did. He say, "That is the woman for me." Oh yes,' as Evelyn made a dissentient movement, 'it was so, and he search and search for you. He tell me all about it. How shocked he was when he did find you and saw the change in you. How he try to help you, but you all prickly like the holly bush. I try to help too. I came to Seefeld to meet you, I ask you here, I make the job for you, so you will not leave Austria, though of course I wanted you myself too, but it was all no good. You care only for that dead man whose affairs were the talk of the Tyrol.'

There was accusation in Sophy's voice. Evelyn could not see her face in the dim bedroom, and she was glad that Sophy could not see hers.

'I so hope you learn to love Max,' Sophy went on, 'he deserves to be loved, and it was so romantic, seeing you in London like that.' ('I do not know which were more ravished, my eyes or my ears,' the words came back to Evelyn). 'He has a picture of you, he wheedled it out of your agent. He show it to me. You were so beautiful, so radiant.'

'That was Evelina Ravelli,' Evelyn said harshly.

'But you are the same. You could be radiant again. He said you were so when he took you to Munich. He had great hopes of that night, since you both love music.'

That night when she had told him she could not forget Harry, but she had done it for the sake of the girl who was pleading with her now.

'You see, Sophy, all along I thought he loved you,' she explained.

'But that was stupid! Surely you could see he thought I was only a child still?' Sophy giggled. 'Me as Max's wife — nein, nein, you are so much more suitable.' (Amy's opinion, Evelyn remembered dryly.) Sophy's voice became coaxing. 'Could you not try to love Max, Eva? You make him so happy.'

'But I do love him.' Almost involuntarily the confession slipped from her. Sophy made a movement of surprise.

'You do? Then have you told him so?'

'No, and I can't, ever. He . . . he doesn't want me any

more. I went to him in the garden, he said some cruel things,' Evelyn's voice faltered into silence as she remembered those things.

'Lovers always seem to be a little cruel to each other,' Sophy said wonderingly. 'It is because he thinks that you do not love him that he says hard things. You must tell him that he is wrong, Eva.'

'Sophy, I can't . . . grovel.'

'You are too proud? Pride is one of the seven deadly sins, Eva, it can cause so much pain. Love should be stronger than pride. I am afraid that Max is proud too, but he is a man, it is the woman who has to . . . what you say . . . grovel.'

Evelyn had been ready to lower her pride in the garden, but before she could say what she had come to say, Max had shattered her with his biting criticisms. 'All you can feel now is appetite.' She could never forgive that, nor could she risk another rejection.

'I think you are letting your romantic fancies run away with you,' she said, with a little forced laugh. 'If ever Max had a yen for me, which I rather doubt, it is over now. You see I am no longer the glamorous Evelina, only her ghost, and at last he has realized it. We have nothing more to say to each other.'

Sophy gave a long sigh, and slipped off the bed.

'Good night, Eva,' she said sadly.

Evelyn was up and dressed soon after it was light. She had not slept. Words and hints Max had uttered kept returning to her. Up on the Karer he had told her he would reveal why he took an interest in her, 'when she was a real woman again', and when he had come to London, he had found a genius, 'and something else.' Poor Max, he had never been able to dissociate her from her legend, and he had tried to recreate her in that glamorous image, but the real woman, Evelyn Rivers, was too changed, and he had been disappointed. It was as simple as that.

Yet there had been moments when he had almost succeeded in recapturing her former self, the drive to Munich, and that interval of time in the music room when they had stood together before the piano and played a duet. Of all her memories that would be the most precious, for then they had been in real communion.

Evelyn left the garden and struck off along the road down the valley away from the town. The mountains were dark blue against the pearly sky, the fields were wet with dew; in some the hay had been cut and stood in conical heaps with a pole through the centre, as was the custom in that country. As yet there was no traffic on the road.

A black and white collie dog was sniffing at the verge. Seeing Evelyn, he looked up and wagged a doubtful tail. She was fond of dogs and held out a hand, and the dog, a friendly animal, received her overtures with rapture. They continued their walk together. Presently the collie ran into a nearby coppice and emerged with a stick which he laid at Evelyn's feet, looking up at her with beseeching eyes. There was no doubt about what he wished her to do with it. She threw it, and he retrieved it. He seemed to have an insatiable appetite for this form of recreation, for Evelyn's arm began to tire long before his enthusiasm waned.

Grown careless since there appeared to be no cars about, she threw it along the road. Too late she saw the vehicle hurtling towards them, driven at furious speed.

It was on the dog before she could do anything about

it. Actually it passed right over him without touching him. The collie decided that the road was no place for him, and tail between his back legs, made a dash for the ditch, blundering against Evelyn in his panic. He knocked her feet from under her, throwing her flat upon her face.

The car slithered to a halt some way on ahead with a squeal of hastily applied brakes, and the driver came running back along the road, uttering imprecations in German. As he reached the prostrate girl, the flood descended upon her. He was, she thought, abusing her for her stupidity in nearly causing him to have an accident. She lay prone, for she had recognized the voice and knew who the driver was. Then she remembered the dog, and lifted her head to look for him.

'*Gott im Himmel*, Eve! What the hell are you doing here at this hour of the morning?'

'The highway is free to all at any hour of the day,' she returned, 'but what happened to the dog?'

Far away across the fields a black and white shape was fleeing.

'He is all right, he could not run like that if he were not. But, Eve,' he knelt down beside her, 'I might have killed you. You are not hurt, are you?'

'You shouldn't have been driving at that reckless speed.'

'And you should not have been wandering about in the middle of the road. Sure you are not hurt?' For she had not attempted to rise.

'I am hurt, terribly hurt,' she told him. 'And it's all your fault!'

She saw his face whiten with anxiety, and was filled with wicked glee. Her hair was cascading over her shoulders, her face and clothes smeared with dust. She saw that

Max did not look much better. The old pullover he was wearing was stained and in places torn, his hair was on end, and he needed a shave.

'Where?' he asked. 'I could have sworn I did not touch you.' He began to move expert fingers over her legs.

'In my heart,' she told him.

He looked up quickly and their eyes met.

'The heart you don't believe I've got,' she added.

'Eve, you little ...!' In his relief he seized her by her shoulders and shook her.

'That won't help,' she gasped. 'Give me a hand up.'

His hands dropped to her wrists, and he pulled her to her feet, but he did not release them.

'Where have you been?' she asked, tossing back her hair. 'You look as if you'd had a night out.'

'So I have, on the mountains. They have always given me great solace.'

'And what did you want solace for?' she queried. 'Sophy's desertion ... or mine?' Her eyes gleamed provocatively.

'Eve, if you look at me like that, I cannot answer for the consequences.'

'That sounds more hopeful,' she told him, her face alight with mischief.

He drew her towards him, until her hands were against his breast, and looking up, she saw flame kindle in his eyes.

'I tried to seduce you once before,' she murmured, 'and I hope the outcome this time will be more satisfactory than the last occasion.'

A slow grin spread over his face.

'I promise you it will be entirely satisfactory to both of us, in fact an Alpine Rhapsody in the style of Franz Liszt, but first there is the little matter of a marriage ceremony, or had you overlooked that?'

'Not entirely, and I was rather hoping it might occur to you.'

'It has been in the forefront of my mind ever since I saw you in London.'

'And that is why you wanted to find Evelina?'

'That is why, and thank God I did find her. Meanwhile, since I am afraid the formalities will take a little time, you can have this on account.'

With a sigh of content she surrendered to his embrace.

The sun came up, touching the mountain summits with gold; traffic began to appear along the road. The disreputable-looking couple by the verge returned to earth and, entwined, walked towards the stationary car.

'It's been a long night,' Evelyn said.

'Yes, but joy cometh in the morning,' Max told her.

FREE!
Harlequin Romance Catalogue

Here is a wonderful opportunity to read many of the Harlequin Romances you may have missed.

The HARLEQUIN ROMANCE CATALOGUE lists hundreds of titles which possibly are no longer available at your local bookseller. To receive your copy, just fill out the coupon below, mail it to us, and we'll rush your catalogue to you!

Following this page you'll find a sampling of a few of the Harlequin Romances listed in the catalogue. Should you wish to order any of these immediately, kindly check the titles desired and mail with coupon.

Have You Missed Any of These Harlequin Romances?

All books are 60c. Please use the handy order coupon.

DD

Have You Missed Any of These
Harlequin Romances?

All books are 60c. Please use the handy order coupon.

EE